Sleeping With Jack Kerouac

A Novel

Sean McGrady

SLEEPING WITH JACK KEROUAC

All Rights Reserved © 2017 by Sean McGrady

Published by Sean McGrady

In memory of my father, and for my sons
Eirik and Bjorn, the next generation –
this is your inheritance,
all of this madness and love and,
yes, heartbreak,
all yours now, take us there.

"Writers aren't people exactly. Or, if they're any good, they're a whole lot of people trying so hard to be one person."
—F. Scott Fitzgerald, *The Love of the Last Tycoon*

"I realized these were all the snapshots which our children would look at someday with wonder, thinking their parents had lived smooth, well-ordered lives and got up in the morning to walk proudly on the sidewalks of life, never dreaming the raggedy madness and riot of our actual lives, our actual night, the hell of it, the senseless emptiness."
—Jack Kerouac, *On the Road*

Sleeping With Jack Kerouac

Prologue

My name is Scotty Dorian, and I am the defendant.

It is almost impossible to believe that I labored for days over that simple, unadorned opening line.

If you are one of those people who still reads newspapers or at least the online aggregates then you know that I'm awaiting trial on first-degree murder charges. For those of you who don't pay attention anymore, and really who can blame you, the state is charging me with the unlawful, willful, and premeditated murder of my husband, Stuart Ogden.

I know it isn't every day that the richly attractive daughter of a renowned publisher murders her literary agent husband in a monumental fit of rage and obsession—all with the supposed and rumored help of her much younger lover, the famous actor-heartthrob in a Netflix series. Let me say, what a strange and chunky sentence that was to cobble together.

It has always been my deepest desire to write a book fine enough to be remembered, and now I finally have the material to warrant such ambition. And the time to do it—these months in prison are for me no different than a residency at Yaddo, a means to achieve the discipline and focus needed to unlock creativity.

They have assigned me to a work detail on the island of the dead. A dozen of us leave Rikers Island each morning and commute by ferryboat to Hart Island, where the city of New York has been burying its anonymous and ignominious, bodies unwanted and unknown, since Civil War days.

On the deck of the boat some of my orange-blazoned colleagues are zoned into the usual mass market drivel, the stamped-out works of Patterson and John Sanford and Higgins Clark, a form of escapism almost entirely lost on me. I try hard not to be a snob in other parts of my life, but books are always going to be a different matter. Now Louisa is devouring the carcass of Stephen King's latest—and I can respect that. King is a decent writer. Louisa looks up at me, her dreadlocks swinging into focus. She still has the nasty shiner from our intimate moment in the shower.

Louisa has learned in a most illiterate way that Tanya has got my back. The six-foot-five-inch former Olympic track star never leaves my side now. Tanya, I should also coincidentally note, has a new publishing deal with Dorian and Cage for a small volume of rap poetry that I judged to be breaking new ground.

My brain is constantly abuzz with ideas for my own work in progress. I'm arrogant enough to believe that the book will practically write itself. Maybe every new author thinks that. Not that there aren't some artistic choices to make—will I opt for the standard first-person narrator or try something fiendishly inventive? Is there a Gatsby-informed neighbor or a hokey *Bright Lights, Big City* second-person device that I should be exploring?

I want to capture it all on paper. I'm so glad for our contemplative time on the water. I love breathing in the sharp winter air, feeling the chop and the spray, inhaling the knowledge that I have not withered and died in vain.

We are nearing the deserted docks of Hart Island. There are over a million dead on the tiny, mile-long parcel of land, and you can feel the mass anguish of that eternal and silent scream—as haunting as the ruins of the ancient women's psychiatric hospital that comes into view.

I'm not sure about "the mass anguish of that eternal and silent scream." It feels a bit forced, a little purply. We'll continue to work on it. I still need to find my true voice. Many writers say that it often takes at least fifty pages before that distinct and idiosyncratic power is jarred loose from the stone like the sword of Excalibur.

I have my doubts about that last sentence, too. I mean, Excalibur—really, Scotty? I remember Twain saying that the difference between choosing the right word and the wrong word is the difference between the lightning bug and the lightning. Writing is so different than editing. My eyes can scan another author's manuscript like a Langley codebreaker, the shape and density of paragraphs no different than their ones and zeros, quick to discover the weakest link of novelistic encryption.

Writing on the blank page is as daunting as undressing a new lover for the first time. I should also say that my book will have plenty of sex—and not that weak tea of *Fifty Shades*, either.

The ferryboat jars up against the rubbered pilings. I scan the joyless faces of my fellow prisoners, as they shove their paperbacks into hip pockets and ready themselves for deboarding, and I can say with confidence that there's not a single one of them who I'd consent to have sex with.

The morning is spent the usual way, hacking at the hard February earth with picks and shovels. We lower perhaps ten to fifteen bodies into the mass grave on any given shift, carefully inventorying the remains and mapping their exact location, in case they have to be dug up at some later date, which happens often enough through order of the court.

Two nonchalant guards with semiautomatic rifles watch over us. They are as grateful for the detail as the prisoners, being in the great outdoors, out of the grim cell blocks of Rikers. I make a game of seeing if I can time their breaks, fantasy playing at what would happen if I were quick enough to topple one of them to snare their weapon and blaze away their lives, all in idle fun.

Just in case you think I'm a psychotic killer I should say at this point that I graduated from Harvard with a Master of Arts in comparative literature, with particular emphasis on twentieth-century American, which meant I spent most of my time with that dusty roster of chalky male privilege who continue to be on trial for unknown offenses in college departments across the land. I don't care what anyone says, I will always love Hemingway and Fitzgerald and O'Hara and Faulkner and Steinbeck and Salinger and Yates and Salter and Updike and Roth and Heller—and all the rest of them—and I won't make apologies for it.

I should also further admit that I served a term at the Iowa Writers' Workshop. I'm reluctant to talk more about it. I will say I wasn't given a fair chance there. They all wanted to cozy up to me because of who my father is. Worse, there was this barely beneath-the-surface hostility, expressed in the envious, solicitous faces of faculty and other students, of *what is she doing here?—why, she doesn't need any help in getting published.*

One of my all-time favorite writers is John Cheever. Ever since my present situation I've been meaning to get my hands on a copy of *Falconer* for a reread. We knew John, of course, and he was a lovely man. It's a shame that his kids and wife couldn't refrain from all that sad gossip after his death. My father and I had the good fortune to visit him up at his lovely home in Ossining one summer afternoon. John was a courtly host. He plied my father with gin and wine and prepared us ham sandwiches on homemade bread for a picnic around the gurgling, natural slate pool he had created in his leafy yard.

I was just a young girl, but Mr. Cheever peppered me with questions that showed genuine curiosity about what it might be like to be me. I was sorry later when so much was made of his drinking and homosexuality. He was a beautiful, tormented artist and he wrote the best short stories of his generation, and for me that is all that will ever matter.

I hope they won't just remember me for the gay sex and the drugs and the frenzied media attention.

I have a new lawyer, and he has never lost a case, which is the way it should be when your fee is four million dollars. I am exhausted by all of it, the depositions and the interrogatories, the leaked emails and text messages, the constant judging from the online, twittering, blogging courtroom that must now qualify as the true postmodern literature of our time.

Unlike the other women I find it hard to free my mind and to enjoy the smell of the loam and the salt marshes. As gulls and cormorants sail constantly overhead, cawing with glee at our fall from grace, we sit Indian style with our lunch on the frostbitten ground, only a few yards from the rude, gaping mouth of the grave. We are bundled in parkas and ski masks, looking more like arctic explorers than inmates.

Today Chef has made us cheese sandwiches, two Kraft singles wedged between slices of oat bread, along with mushy, brown slices of Red Delicious apples.

"I saw you on TV again last night," Brenna says, talking with her mouth full. "That boy and that girl, they really something."

"Now I know why you slaughter your husband," Ariel says. "I kill my man for those pieces of ass. She is yum-yum, even better than that Mr. Jack Kerouac."

I was never one for the novels of Kerouac, and it stays strange to me how large he looms in, what is after all, my story.

"Two bad you ain't going to put your face in that yum-yum sauce anymore," Brenna says, enjoying the banter. "She's somebody else's dessert now."

Their juvenile laughter is tinged with the pointless cruelty of caged humans. I don't bother to look their way or plead my innocence. It will die down eventually.

The Manhattan skyline, pale and jagged, is to our southwest, far enough away to seem mystical and alluring, fraught with past possibility. Closer still are the condominiums and lights of City Island, just a stone's throw to our west. And directly to our north, a short, unbearable few miles up Long Island Sound, is Larchmont, home of Stuart's parents and old, cherished dreams. I wrote the Ogdens multiple times, proclaiming my innocence and deep remorse, but have not heard anything in return, which is not surprising, considering the magnitude of their loss.

My lawyer insists that we need them on our side. Thus far they have not released any statement whatsoever.

As bad as these first weeks have been for me, ripped asunder by the nonnegotiable pain and the absolute unreality of unfolding events, beginning with the knock at the door in the middle of the night and leading in rapid succession to statements and lawyers and being booked and somehow finding myself in manacles, I have not once cried.

The closest I've come to tears was out here on burial duty. For the most part I have no problem with the labor: I just pretend I'm a hired hand on a loading dock, that the coffins are just boxes, heavy with iPads or Kindles from China.

"Easy, easy does it," the women at the top of the hole say the livelong day. "Easy, easy," as they lower the pine boxes down to us for stacking.

The other day, though, we were handling the small boxes, the ones holding the infants and children, life's tiniest paupers and indigents, when somehow one of the coffins slipped through my gloved hands and splintered open to reveal its human contents. It was a baby colored a ghastly purple, its eyes shining blackness at me.

Tanya saw it right away, how stricken I looked, how quickly the tears were gathering. She said, "You do that, I can't protect you. You need to breathe and get past it."

I just made it stop. I forced myself to erase the sonograms of my own pregnancy. That's what I did. I am very determined when I need to be.

We leave the island in twilight, in livid darkness. We sit above deck wearing handcuffs and life preservers. We chug by tugs and barges, by private cruisers and yachts, with the luminous towers and spires of Manhattan lighting our way, ghostly and half-remembered, a place as remote and unreal as Oz. It is always gusty and cold above deck, but tonight the Sound is ripped by violent, unpredictable currents, rocking our little boat with vengeance in her heart.

Waves splash over us and perhaps even threaten to capsize us.

But there are no shouts from the manacled women, no hints of fear—no, nothing easily human like that. I realize I am not scared of drowning, either. All of life is about letting go.

There is more to say. But not now.

I will admit here to a judicious editorial cut; I decided to sever the final page of the prologue. I subscribe to Hemingway's theory of omission. Even if the sentences are gone, you know they were once here, just as an amputee wakes from a dream with a phantom limb, still believing she will walk again. You can still feel it.

Even if the hurtful words and feelings have been decapitated, you know I did not much like my husband at the end.

Chapter 1

I readied myself for the book party. The bedroom windows were open to a gift of a day, the dying warmth of summer still with us even if Central Park was a mad fury of autumnal golds and burgundies, its maples and oaks in full carnal glory.

I felt a self-pitying tinge seeing the vibrator on my nightstand, out in the open. I took it and buried it in the bureau, under the special lingerie I no longer wore. It had almost been a year since Stuart and I had last had sex. Not that I ever wanted to have sex with him again. I wanted him gone from my life. He was dangerous, and my therapist and I had come up with a plan and a timetable, which I was adhering to.

Stuart was in his own bedroom, on the other side of the cavernous apartment, readying himself. I hated that we had to go to this thing together. But the party had been planned for months and it wouldn't have been fair to the author to cancel. Even though I had done my best to steer away from publishing Stuart's clients, I couldn't resist Kent's novel, which brought to mind for me Richard Yates's *A Good School*. The advance reviews were comparing it more to John Knowles's *A Separate Peace*, which I could also see, no different than comparing Valencias to navel oranges.

I had made sure that Sadie was in the apartment today, even if it was normally her day off. Sadie had watched over me since girlhood. I had become a hostage in my own home, the home where I was born, the home of my parents. We Dorians have lived at 1040 Fifth Avenue, a limestone edifice that is one of the city's famous addresses, for over forty years. With the exception of my schooling, this was all I have ever known. For sake of reference, I will turn thirty-nine next week.

I suppose everything is a reference, including my own name, which I quite like. The daughter of F. Scott and Zelda Fitzgerald was called Scotty. My older brother Bumby was named after the son of Ernest and Haley Hemingway. I know this must all sound so screwy to an outsider, but all of it always made perfect sense to me. Let's get this out of the way, too: My father's last name was originally Bromberg. *The Picture of Dorian Gray* was the first novel he ever loved.

I have made no changes to the apartment since my father died three years ago. Why should I? It is comfortable with his vast book collection, the first editions and signed copies of so many dearly departed colleagues, the pursuit of a lifetime, wall to wall, floor to ceiling, all those noble spines reminding me of the happiness we once had. I have not even removed the manuscripts that he was poring over on the night of the final heart attack, they remain preserved and stacked next to his Eames chair in the library, a half-finished bottle of Lagavulin nearby, as was it always.

We were never in the habit of making changes. Even after my mother had run off with the screenwriter, he kept the Danish furnishings she selected and the Hudson River School paintings she was partial to, even though they clashed with his own pop sensibility of Rauschenberg and Hamilton and Katz, and we just never spoke of it, of my mother, of the accident, and it was the same with what happened to Bumby, too.

I would never let Stuart take this place from me, he must have known that. We had a prenup, but my attorneys were not sure I was protected enough, since it wasn't until Dad's death that the apartment, the house in East Hampton, and his stake in the publishing company were fully mine. Stuart would surely come after me, since he was partial to litigation.

Five bedrooms, five marble baths, the original wood flooring from 1930, the ornate moldings, the high ceilings, six working fireplaces, the priceless views of the park—Stuart, I know, had been doing the arithmetic. "How much do you think a place like this would go for in the current market?" he asked, shortly after Dad's funeral.

We met in the no man's land of the living room, under Sadie's watchful eyes. He was dressed in new Brooks Brothers, the way he always seemed to be now, in a sport coat and slacks that seemed picked because they matched the green of his new Mercedes sedan, which I had made the terminal mistake of describing as a hunter green. "Don't be an idiot," he said, "it's Mercedes spruce."

"Ready?" he inquired, studying his own shoes, as if they contained some flaw only visible to him. In fact, they were new chestnut wingtips that would've pleased Gatsby.

Stuart had once been very appealing to me. He was tall and sandy-haired and Waspy, so different from us Dorians, and when we reacquainted at a Harvard Club mixer, I was baited in by his sartorial command and confident, gentlemanly manner. In the courtship phase he overwhelmed me with his pursuit and intoxicated me with his charm and randiness. I had never felt so beautiful or as cherished as I did in those early days. There were signs that something was amiss, but I was not thinking with my head as my father let me know often.

I did not have a deep understanding of what the words narcissist and borderline meant then. How could I possibly have comprehended that this charming man had only pretended to love me, that he lived only in the reflection of my love and devotion to him. Now I belatedly understand that he married me for my good name and reputation and money, these things not surprisingly were of use to him.

I bought a new dress for today's occasion and I had Serge do my hair this morning. In the old days I would feel sexy as we dressed for a party, how many times I nuzzled up to my husband to nibble on his neck and to whisper how handsome he looked. Sometimes even my mild affections would make him explode, not that I ever understood those rageful detonations and what set them off.

We made our way to the lobby without any more talking. Darren hailed us a cab for the short drive downtown.

"Darren, I hope Mary is feeling better. Please give her my best."

"Yes, ma'am, I certainly will," Darren said, holding the door open. "You have a wonderful day, Mr. Ogden and Miss Dorian."

I always tipped the doormen lavishly and treated them with respect, asking after their wives and families. That's how my father taught me. Stuart cringed whenever I engaged with the staff. Today he looked plain angry.

"I can't stand another minute of it," he said.

"That makes two of us."

We were silent after that as God tormented us still with a cab that hit every single red light on what would normally be a quick, short ride to the Seagram Building.

"I'm sure you've forgotten," Stuart said, "but my parents' fiftieth anniversary is tomorrow and you are expected to make an appearance."

I didn't think I had the stamina for any more of this charade. I wanted this over. My life was in mortal danger, whether anyone else believed that or not.

"We'll bring Susan, too," Stuart said, as if he anticipated my safety concerns.

Susan Ogden was Stuart's partner in the literary agency. That her last name was the same as Stuart's was just strange coincidence. They had met in law school. They formed the agency, Ogden and Ogden, after Stuart had finally called it quits on his own aborted literary career. Stuart had tried his hand at a series of legal thrillers that were published in mass market paperback but which had failed to excite anyone, including his wife.

Ogden and Ogden handled a diverse group of authors, but Stuart's specialty was crime and detective fiction. The agency had prospered this past year when the estate of Leo Gross, the deceased author of over thirty best-selling police procedurals featuring Lieutenant Joseph Reaper, discovered a cache of three unpublished novels in the attic of Gross's Montauk house.

"Going to Frankfurt for the book fair next week," Stuart said at the last red light. "Wanted to make sure you remembered."

Remembered? Why, that was the plan. I would get the restraining order then. Move his things into storage. I would've changed the locks, too, but we didn't have locks at 1040 Fifth Avenue.

I couldn't get out of the taxi fast enough.

The party was in full swirl by the time we entered the Grill Room. Stuart, thank god, left me immediately to find his author. The head count was good, over a hundred guests plucking crab cakes and smoked salmon off the shouldered silver trays. You have no doubt been to the Four Seasons, I'm sure, a tourist taking in the walnut paneling, the iconic Phillip Johnson design, the floor-to-ceiling windows, the undulation of those crazy coppery and silvery chain curtains, all that majestic mid-century sweep. To me it was homey. I felt the same way about the Rainbow Room or the 21 Club. These were the living rooms where our friends gathered dozens of times a year to celebrate publishing success.

I went all out for this one. I know some of the houses are counting their pennies, but I wanted to make sure that it was known that Dorian and Cage had no such worries. And we didn't. Our back catalog was the envy of many much larger houses, houses owned by media companies and German conglomerates, so strong that even the gangsters at Amazon played nice with us, with our carefully cultivated list of National Book Award and PEN/ Faulkner winners championed early on by Martin Cage, then the authors that my father had diligently courted and collected all across Europe who would go on to find critical and mass success in the US and in some cases make it all the way to Stockholm.

We did not have to publish many new novels from unknowns anymore, but when we did we paid solid advances and worked diligently to create the needed publicity to get the books on the shelves of remaining bookstores and to create the powerful illusion of trending on social media.

Lizza Morris, our chief of publicity, was air traffic control, bringing our VIP guests in for landing and directing them to the coat room, drinks, tables, and to the comfort of other well-heeled guests whom she knew they might know. She spotted me right off and swiped a flute of champagne off a tray for me and was almost instantly beside me.

"What's the score?" I said, taking a deep, calming swig of the drink.

"Kent's in the Pool Room, surrounded by the downtown crowd. Graydon Carter made it. Gay Talese and Tom Wolfe are at four o'clock. Malcolm Gladwell brought half the editorial staff of the New Yorker. Governor Cuomo's here—I don't know who invited him. The actor Jake Gyllenhaal has been a mensch, the photographers won't leave him alone."

"Smart boy, he's protecting his investment," I said, knowing how much Jake had to put down for the film rights.

"Some of his A-list friends will be joining him shortly," Lizza said without the predatory joy she usually got from such news.

Lizza was in a smart, little black cocktail dress and her blonde bob was frosted to perfection. Still, even with the right coiffure and right couturier, she appeared wannish and discontented, as if there was some larger dissatisfaction to be found beneath the accomplished surface.

"What's the matter?" I said, finishing off the champagne.

"My marriage," she said. "Mara told me she's leaving me. Lovely. That's not the worst of it."

I waited. "All along she's been seeing this slam poet from Brooklyn," she said finally. "I'm such a fool. She says I'm too vanilla. Marriage equality to divorce equality."

"What can I do?" I asked Lizza, thinking back to their lovely ceremony on Nantucket less than six months ago.

"I know you can give me the name of a good divorce attorney," she said, privy to my own circumstances. "I just need to get through this launch party. You go now. You have people who want to talk to you. Marty's been looking for you, too."

Lizza pointed to Martin Cage, who held the other fifty percent of our privately held enterprise, who was chatting with the novelist Donna Tartt and her agent, Amanda Urban, by the oyster bar that had been set up for the party.

Marty was more than just a business partner, he was practically family, our oldest and dearest friend, in his late seventies now, an old lion who was sadly losing his roar. He appeared frailer than ever, holding onto his cane for balance, his face gaunt even if that full, preposterous head of silver hair remained. Marty pointed to the oysters and motioned me over.

"Try the Hama Hama," he said, slurping one down. "A river in Washington state. I had to ask."

"Binky, Donna," I said, greeting the bestselling author and her power agent with European air kisses. "Wonderful that you could come."

Ms. Tartt, a very fine and reclusive writer who usually steers clear of such spectacle, said, "I hate to disagree with Marty, but I prefer our local blue points."

"I'm partial to the local oysters, too," I said. "And the local talent. Thanks so much for the advance blurb."

"Kent's novel is very promising," Donna said, "it is the least I can do."

Marty said, "You'll never guess what we were talking about before you scooted over here?"

Binky said, "It's a party, Marty—why ruin it?"

Marty, undeterred, said, "The word in the room tonight is that we're in play. That we want to sell the company and that the party is a show for the money set."

"I didn't know that Pacific Northwest oysters had hallucinogenic effects," I said, trying to make light of it. "I did know about the mushrooms out there."

The three remained eager-faced and quiet, waiting for more.

"Don't you think I'd know if we were selling?" I said, with just a jigger too much of being caught off guard.

"You really should try the Hama Hama," Marty said again, slurping back another.

"I want to go see the birthday boy," I said, taking my leave. "A first novel is just like being born into the world for the first time."

I didn't pause for oysters or the ahi sliders or any of the rest of it. I ate earlier, knowing that it was my job as hostess to look after others, to give each wondrous person here 120 seconds of lavish praise and dutiful love. And that was easy because there wasn't a person in the room who had not done something extraordinary to earn their place here this evening.

I lifted another flute of champagne from yet another silver tray, as I worked my way to the Pool Room. I tilted it back as if I was downing a shot of whiskey before exchanging quick hellos with some of my authors. Authors is an encompassing term when describing a former mob boss, a best-selling psychotherapist, and a real-life female private eye who Chandler might've invented if he lived now.

"Where's that no-good husband of yours?" asked Carlo Bassi good-naturedly. "You just say the word—and I'll have him whacked."

Georgie Guns, which is not her birth name, laughed heartedly. "Be careful of Stuart," the buxom-flaunting PI said, winking at me. "There's a killer inside of that one for sure."

I exchanged knowing looks with Dr. Joyce Rock, my therapist and the author of the number one book on the current *Times'* nonfiction list, *The Narcissist-Borderline Outbreak*.

Georgie, a hard-drinking, chain-smoking, thrice-married military veteran, had a series of hardcore noirs featuring Detective Nicoal Angel. And Carlo Bassi, the Armani-attired mafioso, his silver hair barbered daily, who was widely rumored to have killed or ordered to their deaths at least two dozen men, had written without the help of a ghostwriter a deeply-felt, multigenerational novel set in Queens about a fictional and quite dysfunctional mob family that bore more than a passing resemblance to his own.

"I love this lady," Carlo said, putting a strong arm around me. "She's beautiful and smart. A great editor."

"You just say that because I didn't change a word to your manuscript. I was too scared to. I was afraid you'd have me whacked."

"I can't believe she's not Italian," he said, undaunted. "The dark hair, the olive skin, the great figure. I even love her name. Scotty Dorian. It made me recently try out a little F. Scott Fitzgerald."

"My parents also considered naming me Brett from *The Sun Also Rises.*"

"Today they'd probably name you Katniss Everdeen," Georgie said, cackling.

"Or else Hermione Granger," Dr. Joyce said. "I was so glad when my children got old enough to read for themselves and I didn't have to Harry Potter it anymore."

"That lady's a billionaire," Carlo said, letting go of me. "I got to put some wizards and crazy flying broomstick games in my next novel."

"If you do, I'll have to edit for sure," I said, taking my leave. "So great seeing all of you tonight—and knowing that my amazing writers are becoming fast, new friends to each other."

I wondered if I'd ever make it to the Pool Room. Another passing tray of champagne flutes. Another quickie.

"I see what you're up to," said a male voice from behind me. "It's your party and you can get drunk if you want to."

I turned around to periscope a very handsome young man in a woolen lumberjack shirt and chinos. He stood out from the crowd from being so underdressed for the occasion.

"Who was it that said that out of the last seven American Nobel Prize winners in literature that six of them were alcoholic and the other one wasn't very good anyway?"

"Are you suggesting that I'm alcoholic? Besides, I'm quite

fond of Toni Morrison."

"I'm suggesting we belong to a profession that encourages a certain leniency in that direction."

"I don't believe I know you," I said, sticking out my hand to shake. "'I'm Scotty Dorian."

"Everyone knows who you are," the handsome stranger said, bowing, and then regally taking my hand and kissing the back of it. "I'm Jack Kerouac from Lowell, Massachusetts."

"Are you some relation to the author?" I said, not quite taking it in. The strange thing was that he looked like the early, vigorous Jack Kerouac from those long-ago, glossy jacket sleeves.

"I'm sorry but I *am* Jack Kerouac. I wrote *On the Road*. I'm the king of the Beats."

I became aware of a small crowd of guests beginning to hover around us, their attention clearly focused on Jack.

"But Kerouac is dead," I felt compelled to say.

"What do you think of my work?" he demanded.

"Well, quite frankly," I said, finding my wits about me, "I've never really gone for all that stream-of-consciousness, unpunctuated paper reaming. Wasn't it Capote who said, 'That's not writing, that's *typing*.'"

"You're just unnerved by my potent virility," he said. "You can feel the fucking in me in every sentence."

I was unnerved by him; his blue eyes seemed to burrow in and to penetrate me. The small crowd was forming a line, politely waiting their turn to talk to this stranger.

Suddenly he let out a bellowing laugh. "You don't watch television, do you, Miss Dorian?"

"We've never owned one," I said.

"I'm the Jack Kerouac starring in the Netflix series *Off the Road*. I'm a friend of Jake Gyllenhaal's, he invited me tonight."

"Oh, that explains it," I said, clearly sounding relieved. "What's your real name then?"

"It really is Jack." He turned to the waiting line, then turned back to me. "Be careful not to overindulge tonight, Scotty."

The moment I was out of range I helped myself to another drink. Who in the world does he think he is, I thought. Jack Kerouac, my ass.

We had set Kent up with a table, alongside the gurgling fountain in the Pool Room, to sign copies of his novel. He looked flush with his newfound success, smiling and shaking hands with the swells who were now his new admirers. Stuart stood next to him, looking as glum as a sentry at Buckingham. I wondered why Susan Ogden was not in attendance.

It was still a thrill to publish a novel. Every new novel carries with it a secret hope to be the one, that rare beauty that sets the country's heart aflutter, a book to be remembered for and that will guarantee the author, as my father amusedly like to say, a table at 21 and an obit in the *Times*.

First novels were even better. They were all about beginnings. Beginnings to long, nourishing careers. Beginnings to a certain kind of literary life that brought with it storied friendships with editors and agents and other authors. And with each successive novel, the hope remained the same, secret and eternal, that this could be the one to set you free.

With books and writers you never knew. Many good books never find traction. Many fine writers die unheralded. I've published many first-rate novels that did not do what I thought they would do. Good and fine and first-rate are not enough. Greatness is what eludes us, and I grew up firmly believing that all a writer has to do in this lifetime was write one great novel. If you did that, it did not matter what a mess you made of your life otherwise; if you were able to write one for the ages then all manner of personal transgression was forgiven.

I thought of Fred Exley who wrote *A Fan's Notes*. He would write only two more novels, neither as good, not that I didn't respect *Pages From a Cold Island*, and his life finally belonged to the bartenders, one vodka tonic after another. My father and I made a pilgrimage to see the great man on Alexandria Bay, a couple of years before Fred finally succumbed. I must've been about thirteen, and we took a fishing trip. Fred was sloppy and slurry from a cooler's worth of Molsons. I remember that he was very intent on learning my opinion of the newswoman Diane Sawyer's backside. "Scotty," he asked, "what do you think of Diane's ass? I think it's a natural wonder of the world but I'm open to second opinions."

Fred had written a great novel, though, and we would as likely make fun of him as a Sardinian peasant would ridicule the pope.

Kent's novel was most decent but it was nowhere near exalted. The hope was that we were beginning a career—in fact, we had already contracted him for two more books. Kent was dressed stylishly in a wide-striped Thomas Pink shirt and a pinstriped Zegna suit—he had emailed me what he was going to wear—along with sapphire-framed eyeglasses and a shiny, large chronograph taking up new residency on his wrist. He was lean and tall and still sinewy at age twenty-six. He was also gay and black and photogenic and very quotable. To ice this literary confection, Kent had recently emerged triumphantly from rehab, ending his addiction to OxyContin, which he ingested with shots of Wild Turkey, and which he declared in the latest issue of *Poets & Writers* as the gateway that allowed his words to soar to stratospheric heights—believe it or not, this was most excellent publicity in our cloistered world.

I was tapped on the shoulder by Lannigan Sinclair. "Thrilling find," he said, wobbling on his feet and sounding very much drunk.

Lannigan had been a much-photographed man about town who'd gone on to start the careers of several notorious, coke-sniffing writers who were all the rage at the end of the last century. He had been as well known for his long, shaggy blond hair and Odeon-partying days as he was for discovering talent. The night crawling and lost decades had caught up with Lannigan, leaving him ashen and cadaverous, as if he was already in transition from this world to the next.

"What is all this shit anyway?" Lannigan said, turning on me and holding up Kent's book, *The Fields of Play*. "You know, this isn't exactly like starting the career of a Jimmy Baldwin. I thought you seers at Dorian and Cage were better than this."

Before I could rally a defense, he put his spectacles on, took another unneeded sip of whiskey, and read sneeringly from the book-jacket copy:

"'Quentin Marsh is the headmaster at Margate, a very private and exclusive all-boys prep school in a small New Hampshire town in the shadow of the White Mountains. Marsh's tranquil, quiet life is suddenly awakened, though, by the arrival of Rudd Dakota, an enigmatic young African American with a mysterious past. Dakota immediately captures the attention of the upper-crust Margate community with his winning maneuvers on the rugby field and his Southern, genteel ways. Even Quentin Marsh, long insulated from his true inner self, emerges from fitful slumber in this remarkable debut.'"

"That's just book-jacket copy," I said. "The novel is beautifully written and realized."

"Spare me," Lannigan said. "You're just going after the gay reader block, just admit it. This is nothing but a tender piece of pornography, a softcore ode to boys in shorts and the boarding schools that provided the communal showers."

"That is so not fair, Lannigan. When did you become such a homophobe? Kent's work has appeared in *Ploughshares* and *Paris Review* and—"

Lannigan suddenly pointed to Kent and Stuart and said: "So who do you think is buggering whom? My money is on the tall blond one. His face is without empathy. I've seen him somewhere before."

"I beg your pardon—"

"Come on now, Scotty. Don't play Louisa May Alcott with me. You know what I'm talking about—who's taking it up the ass? Because somebody's got to fuck and somebody's got to get fucked. That's just the way the world works."

"For your information, Lannigan, the tall, blond man with the face without empathy is my husband, Stuart."

"Whoever. Whatever. You must be living in a cave or a dream or both. You know less than nothing."

"At least I'm not a lunatic," I said.

"Fuck you and the horse you rode in on," the once-famous editor said before departing.

Chapter 2

We took the spruce Mercedes sedan. We could've hailed a cab, or a town car, or Ubered it, of course. But Stuart relished pulling into the Larchmont Yacht Club in his new toy, acting as if it was nothing to plunk down 100 K on an armored tank. I never learned to drive, being a city girl, and Stuart liked to hold that over me, because that's what narcissist sickos do.

So Stuart drove, and Susan Ogden sat in the passenger seat, which was my wont. I pretended to be busy with my iPhone in the back. Please, I prayed, don't start a conversation with me. Only thirty-nine minutes with current traffic to Larchmont, according to Google maps.

"I hear from everyone that Kent's launch party was a smash," Susan said, oblivious.

I should tell you a few things about Susan right now, before we go on any longer. Susan used to be a man named Mallon. I liked Mallon, and I like Susan. The change didn't take as long to get used to post-op as I thought it might. There was the occasional slip with the pronouns but nothing that wasn't recoverable from.

The first couple of years after her metamorphosis Susan seemed to all of us released from her bondage, giddy with her new wardrobe and the freedom to be her true self. Susan and I sometimes shopped together at Bergdorf's, and her sense of style was so much more attuned than my own. I kept it simple, grays and blacks from Klein and Karan, but she took chances, striking reds and yellows from Valentino, unafraid to don a leopard-print scarf or high-heel Manolos.

Susan was tall and statuesque, and she kept her hair colored lemony blond and shoulder-length. I admired her confident, long stride when she entered a room and how she seemed always able to bring out the best in Stuart. She was his other wife, as much a part of Stuart's life as I was, and in some ways they actually spent more time together, all those eleven-hour days at the office, building their client lists and their reputation at Ogden and Ogden.

I often wondered how Susan was able to tame Stuart. Did she also witness his strange, out-of-nowhere explosions of rage? How could she have not noticed his constant need to win, to come out on top of every conversation, the way even morning coffee talk became gladiator blood sport? Did he chip away at her esteem, little by little, bit by malevolent bit, as he had done with me? Did he gaslight her reality, too?

At least she did not have to sleep with him. Not that I did that anymore, either. I could not please him, that is the simple truth, in bed or anywhere else. He needed things to be done just so, in the most controlling of ways, and if they were not done just so, he would savagely berate me. I had been reduced to tears so many times, and the fool that I am kept blaming myself and wondering what I was doing wrong. It wasn't until I found Dr. Joyce that the veil began to lift.

Stuart couldn't stand that I had sought out therapy. He demanded to know why I needed to see Joyce, and it necessitated a lie on my part: I told him I was having such a difficulty getting over my father's death that I needed to speak to someone. This explanation only pacified him temporarily. Of course his sociopathic tendencies made it difficult for him to even understand a thing like true grief. I remember the way he examined me at my father's funeral, working hard to understand all those tears. The only time I ever saw Stuart even look slightly wet-eyed was at the service for crime novelist Elmore Leonard.

Now I worried for Susan. Now that I was increasingly absent

from Stuart's life, indeed actively plotting my escape, was Susan getting her own glimpses of the monster? In the last months I had watched as she became unaccountably and noticeably gloomy, even as their agency was prospering with its newly discovered Leo Gross manuscripts.

I did not text people unless it was a matter of some urgency, so when my phone made that awful trumpeting note, my first reaction was alarm. It was also partly the post traumatic stress I always felt from having received so many texts from Stuart, which purported to be loving but which were really another means of control, as he sought to know my whereabouts at all times of the day.

The text blurb said: "Jack Kerouac here, let's meet for a cocktail this evening. I know you like drinks and I know you like books. I have a novel you might be interested in."

A second later another blurb was trumpeted: "Don't blame Jake—got your number from him."

Jack could not have wooed me in a worse way. Texting was the first and last resort of a coward. To my way of thinking a gentleman makes a phone call and has the courage for a real ask. Jack's novel was probably some experimental tripe written all in tweets and texts. He could never imagine how many people wanted me to read their books, anyway.

I said to the car, "Jack Kerouac made an appearance at Kent's party."

"Have you seen *Off the Road?*" Susan said brightly. "It's great, highly stylized the way *Mad Men* was, capturing the fifties and sixties in suburban America through the crazy lens of Kerouac, Ginsberg, and Burroughs."

"Scotty doesn't watch television," Stuart said. "She's a scroll-and-parchment kind of gal."

"Kerouac is quite the stud in the show, beds down men and women left and right," Susan said. "The show is a hot, bubbling caldron of bisexuality."

"Oh, did you all hear about Lannigan Sinclair?" Stuart said cheerily, changing the subject. "There was an item in *Huffpo*. The news had just come in. Not sure what the full story is, but Lannigan hanged himself this morning."

"Oh, my God," I gasped. "I was talking to him last night."

"Maybe that's what did the poor man in," Stuart cracked.

"It was out there that he wasn't in a good way," Susan said. "I heard from one of his fellow editors that he had been suffering through a bad love affair."

"Aren't we all," Stuart said under his breath.

Susan said, "It seems he was seeing one of his male novelists. And the novelist cut it off."

"His heyday was long in the rearview," Stuart concluded.

The tears were gushing down my cheeks. Poor Lannigan. He had been a brave, great editor once. In his prime he had the discernment and energetic enthusiasm to usher into print some wonderful young talent that we were all the better for having read. I was thinking particularly of several minimalist short story writers whom I so admired, and I knew better than most what unabated efforts it took to convince your fellow editors to launch somebody new and the relentless advocacy required for successful publishing splashdowns. Even death could never, ever take that away from Lannigan.

Susan checked back on me and glimpsed my wet cheeks. "Are you all right, Scotty? I didn't realize you had known Lannigan so well."

"It's not that," Stuart answered for me. "Suicides, that's what does it. It makes her think of Bumby."

The yacht club, moored on the perennial gray waters of Long Island Sound, was an Ogden family institution, where all anniversaries and birthdays were commemorated, where Stuart's father Thaddeus was better known as Commodore Ogden. Of course Commodore Ogden had never been in the navy—instead he served as the head of a giant hedge fund bearing his own name, a name that had made it, embarrassingly enough, into one of Michael Lewis's Wall Street exposes.

The club was a white-shingled, green-shuttered wedding cake on a protected inlet, with enough docking to accommodate the yachts, schooners and cruisers that had to be of a certain length and cost to qualify for membership. Larchmont was the kind of affluent bedroom community, seemingly removed from the wild vicissitudes of Manhattan, that John Cheever liked to set his stories in, everything proper and in its place on the surface and yet just below pure, hateful madness.

There was a large turnout to celebrate the Ogdens' marital and financial longevity. Thaddeus and his wife, Lucinda, were at one of the circular tables surrounded by well-wishers; I would have to figure a way to sneak in a quick, inauthentic greeting. In the meantime I made my determined way to the open bar.

Thaddeus and Lucinda begot five sons, who were all—with the exception of Stuart—what Tom Wolfe used to call masters of the universe. These lackluster men of finance were all in dutiful attendance today, as well as their unemancipated wives and their Facebook-addled children, who all seemed well on their way to a lifetime of drug addiction and rehab. I shouldn't speak, of course, as I asked for two dirty Hendrick's martinis from the stiff in white tails minding the bar. I downed one of them in two absurd gulps and left the empty glass behind.

The rich, glowing, Waspy faces looked at home in the club's nautical interior, which was like the inside of a luxury liner, gleaming with brass and polished teak, replete with fancy directional instruments and decorative oars and ship's wheels. I found a lonely corner by the large stone fireplace, which was ablaze, to sip my second martini in peace. I began to clench up in sadness calling up Lannigan again. And, as much I didn't want to admit it, it brought up Bumby and the whole awfulness of Ketchum, Idaho.

At least Lannigan, Bumby, and I belonged to a tribe that

pursued a dream I could readily make sense of. I looked around at the well-dressed, well-behaved guests of Commodore Ogden, and they were of a sort, pleasant but noncommittal about politics and the arts, their bland, self-assured faces reflecting back the knowledge that money is the only pursuit worth having, a sense of mystification that others weren't fully able to grasp something so elemental as that. I heard snippets of conversations about newly purchased country homes in Tuscany and the Loire Valley, of new Lear jet refinements and overpriced Picassos, of ambassadorships that would soon be up for grabs with the new administration, a world unthinkable enough that even our best fiction writers are challenged to conjure wealth and influence on this scale.

Of course in one very important way, I was a hypocrite, since I had the money to gain entrance to this Faustian club. It was also true that top editors like Lannigan lived their own life of privilege, not that it was spoken of, supping in reviewed restaurants—still able to partake in hoary, afternoon-extinguishing two-martini lunches—getting away to their country places up the Hudson or out on the East End, sheltered in the hallowed pursuit of discovering the next important voice, the long weekend spent with a tall pile of braided manuscripts that had been messengered in by the literary agents on Thursday—along with the PDF versions for the younger editorial set who were more at home scanning would-be greatness on an iPad—try explaining that decadence to any hard-earning waitress or plumber.

Stuart's brother Henry and his wife Allison were the first to spot me and make their way over. Henry was dressed like he had finished first at Augusta, in one of his marvelously obscene lime jackets from J. Press, while Allison was relying on pink angora and a festive assortment of hair ribbons to get her through the middle years.

"Scotty, is it true that Dorian and Cage is up for sale?" Henry asked, skipping the preamble.

Henry worked in arbitrage, not that I fully understood it. All I knew was he was a partner at Loveless, Greed & Vicious and that his face had recently stared back at me from the cover of *Fortune* with the header: "The Vanquisher."

"You shouldn't do a thing without my assistance," he pursued.

I didn't know what to say to this so like a true bitch I said sweetly, "Henry, would you be a dear and fetch me another Hendrick's martini?"

That left me uncomfortably alone with Allison. She was one of those immaculate, floral-fresh women who run their households like they are competitive, money-making endeavors. It should be said her households were mansions in Greenwich and Southhampton. She also had a line of cosmetics, not that anyone knew what qualified her for such a thing, after all she was not a rare beauty nor was she known for breaking down chemical compounds. The very rich often achieve their dreams simply because they treat their dreams as if they are nothing so out of the ordinary as, say, eyeing color swatches for the grand hall.

"I wish Henry was dead," Allison said.

A pianist was tinkling the ivories to Cole Porter standards, as the club continued to fill up with life's happy winners.

"Do you think you can get me in contact with Dr. Joyce Rock?" Allison asked. "I read her book, and I desperately need to talk to her. I am tired of living with Henry and his narcissism."

I stood there mute, knowing that it was too late in my relationship with Allison to befriend her and utter truth.

"He hasn't let me see my family in years," she said. "It's so insidious. They break you down, wear you out. Narc vampires, always looking for their next transfusion. You're lucky you don't have children. Once you have them, there's no way out."

Henry returned with my drink. "I'll get you that number," I told Allison.

"What were you all talking about?" he said.

"You," Allison said. "Isn't that what you want to hear?"

He shrugged it off and turned back to me. "You'll be seated next to us at dinner. It's all arranged. We can talk then about next steps."

"I'd rather die than sell," I said.

Without another word I took my drink and headed for the safety of the outdoor patio. I had come out in time to witness the sunset, the warm pinks and oranges melting into the Sound, layered like a Rothko, a suicide of abstract color.

Bumby blew his brains out with a shotgun in the same house in Ketchum that Hemingway did the deed in. He would've used the same double-barreled shotgun—he said so in his diary, *Notes From Above Ground*, which my father published posthumously— but Mary Hemingway had had it melted down.

Poor, sweet Bumby—he was a better writer than he knew. He felt he had failed all of us. All he ever wanted to do was write something good. Even our own mother, who'd been an Elite model, had finished a novel that had been respectfully reviewed.

By now I was weepy with the drink and the memories. I missed my brother and my mother and my father. I was all alone in the world. There was no one to take my calls anymore on those long Sunday afternoons of the soul, when most of us make that list of what true friends we have left.

I could make out Stuart's young nieces and nephews copping a smoke by the docks, in their navy blazers and tartan skirts, with all their ruddy-faced, mussy-haired entitlement, looking like an advertisement for Ralph Lauren and that thinly imagined American dream. In the far distance, the city remained in sight, a phantasm of the early evening, the replaced tower of One World Trade Center glowing like a raised fist through Gotham's silhouette.

The music wafted through the open French doors, this time the pianist was singing "Night and Day." I couldn't help but think it was the dying music of a vanishing civilization. I turned to look back inside the club and I could see the tables being readied for dinner. I was also surprised to see that Kent was on the list for the anniversary party. He was by the bar with Susan and they seemed to be having some kind of serious exchange of words, to judge by their postures and the cowering of nearby guests.

I had to leave at once. The only question was whether to sneak away without saying my goodbyes. Stuart would be furious, of course, and I would have to speak to him in that preposterously calm and childlike way that Joyce advised. *I'm sorry that makes you feel that way, Stuart. It must not feel good to feel that way. Your feelings matter to me. Let's discuss this later at home when we're calmer.*

I remembered Sadie wasn't going to be in the apartment tonight—I needed to check into a hotel, leave nothing to chance. In the morning Stuart would fly to Frankfurt. Tomorrow I would begin a new life. It had been years since I possessed such tremulous hope for things that other people surely took for granted, to sleep deeply without the constant fear of him, to wake refreshed in the morning, stretching my arms unguardedly, the tall windows open to the fragrant breezes of possibility.

Again I saw Stuart standing over our bed with the scissors and felt the familiar geysers of shame for allowing this intruder in. This was not the book I intended to write with my life.

I decided to duck out using the outdoor walkway. I turned one final time to the warm yellow light coming through the doors of the club and caught the surreal scene of Susan throwing a drink in Kent's face.

Chapter 3

After stopping at the apartment to pack an overnight bag, I checked into the Alqonquin, it's where my father and I would always stay when we were having renovations done.

Feeling an old-fashioned hunger, I ordered filet mignon and a Caesar salad from room service, with a half liter of cabernet. Afterward, I took a long shower, to give myself the time to properly think it through, and then after I toweled off and put on a robe and was unable to change course I texted Jack Kerouac to meet me in the hotel bar.

In my office I have a framed manuscript page from Annie Lamott's wise incantation, *Bird by Bird*. I no longer remember who gifted it to me, but it is the page where she distills E. L. Doctorow's advice for writing and living. "Writing a novel is like driving a car at night," she quotes Doctorow as saying. "You can see only as far as the headlights, but you can make the whole trip that way."

I didn't know what I was inviting in with Jack, but I figured to be just fine if I kept to the headlights and what was right in front of me.

When I came down, Jack was waiting for me at the gleaming bar, holding the stool next to him vacant with his tweed jacket. He was bathed in blue light, blue from the ceiling, blue from the bar and the bottles, blue blue blue. Frank Sinatra sang about the summer wind.

The boy was seriously beautiful, the wavy black hair, the face of an Abercrombie model, his rolled-up sleeves articulating powerful biceps.

He rose to greet me. "I'm glad for this, Scotty."

He smelled good. A woodsy, smoky scent with just the faintest notes of citrus and mojito, I thought like a deviant sommelier, already uncorking him. Up close his eyes were like coals burning a blue flame, heated down to their essence.

He summoned the red-jacketed barkeep. Next to his tumbler glistening with melting ice was a trade paperback edition of *Naked Lunch*, which was resting atop a rather thick-looking, homemade manuscript.

I quipped the Robert Benchley line, "Let's get out of these wet clothes and into a dry martini."

"The house martini it is," he told the bartender. "And another one for me," he said, pointing to his emptied drink. When the red jacket turned his attention to the bottles, Jack said, "The bar menu has that quote of Benchley's. And a few more by Dorothy Parker. All those dead, vicious legends of the round table."

"We knew Benchley's grandson, the novelist who wrote *Jaws*. We'd see him from time to time out on the East End at some afternoon lawn party. He was a struggling, languishing newspaperman for quite a long while before his ultimate success. I always felt sorry for him. So much to live up to. Maybe I was just feeling sorry for myself."

The drinks came, and we clinked glasses. He said, "One day I will find the right words, and they will be simple. Cheers."

"Who said that?"

"Well, I did. It's from *Dharma Bums*."

"*It all ends in tears, anyway*. Didn't you also write that in *Dharma Bums*?"

"I didn't know you were a fan."

"I'm not. One of my writers used it for his novel's epigraph." I pointed to the amber fluid in his glass. "What are you drinking?"

"Canadian Club whisky. I'm remaining in character. Kerouac liked beer with chasers of CC. He always had a hidden flask of the stuff, even when he went into the bars. Bartenders didn't much like him because of it. Jack thought it was funny."

"He died of the drink, right?"

"Was drinking whisky in the morning down in Florida and eating a tuna sandwich when he started coughing up blood. He was an old man of forty-seven."

"How awful," I said, stabbing at the plump olive at the bottom of my glass.

Jack called down to the bartender for two more. He said, "I like this place, it fits you."

"I thought downtown was more to your liking. Some Village jazz club maybe, or the White Horse Saloon where Dylan Thomas died from eighteen shots of whisky. And what do you mean by saying this place fits me?"

"You remind me of a character in a Wes Anderson film. Do you even know who he is? It's just that there is something refined and idiosyncratic about you. Or maybe to put it in a way you would better understand, you are like one of those beautiful and not readily seen souls in an Anita Brookner novel—"

"Anita Brookner? I can't believe you've read Brookner."

"My father is a movie producer, he optioned one of her books. He wanted my opinion. Anyway, that's not the point. You're sexy and classy, that's all I'm trying to say."

It had been a long time since a man had spoken to me with such directness. He was inches from me, and we held eyes for a long, not uncomfortable moment before letting go.

He said, "I also learned from the menu jottings that this is the very building where the *New Yorker* came into existence."

"They still put the latest issue in the hotel rooms. I was glad to see it tonight. Traditions are important."

"You're staying at the hotel?"

"I'm having a personal renovation done."

He looked at me quizzically. "Ms. Scotty Dorian, I know, among many other things, that you are married."

"Oh, I hate this search engine world," I spilt out. "I remember when people actually met and talked to each other and information flowed naturally from the source."

"Trouble at home?"

"F. Scott Fitzgerald believed that you could become spiritually and emotionally bankrupt, no different than a financial bankruptcy. The emotional capital just runs out, if you don't hold anything in reserve. Well, the same thing happens to marriages. There is only so much good will and capital in any one thing."

"I assume Fitzgerald is your favorite writer because of your name."

"He's great, but my favorite writer is, shockingly, Irwin Shaw. I've never told anyone that. It's my secret shame. *The Young Lions* is my favorite novel. I'm sure it's out of print."

"I've never heard of Irwin Shaw."

"How old are you, anyway?"

"Twenty-eight—and you'd know that if you'd done your Google homework."

"I'm a decade closer to the grave than you. You're part of that generation that just stays at home and swipes through an app to find your soulmate."

"You're sounding as old as Dorothy Parker right now."

"Who are your favorite writers, other than Jack Kerouac?"

"Bukowski, Hunter S. Thompson, Don DeLillo, Cormac McCarthy..."

"That's a strong, masculine list," I said, content with his choices.

In the crowded blue swirl we began to stare into each other's eyes, and that was all there was and all that I can remember. He put his hand on my leg and pulled me closer to him. The words stopped and it was just that deep and trashy stare for meaning, just close-ups of pupils and irises.

We started to kiss in that crazy blue disco light. We kissed hungrily, scraping teeth and biting lips, like it had been a long time between meals for the both of us. I have no idea how long we were at it.

Soon we were getting up from our stools and Jack was paying the check. Then we were crossing the lobby and getting into an elevator. And we were moving up floors as if in a dream.

I kept thinking, it's okay, we're just driving. Just what's in your headlights, don't worry about how the journey ends.

I keyed the door to my room. I've read this moment many times in many books, but it had never played out like this for me. There was always something in me that would hesitate and not allow myself such unstructured submission. Wild abandon was for the literary hacks of the world.

We shed clothes so quickly that it wasn't quite clear who was taking off what from whom. He threw me on the bed, and I guided him to me. Just glimpses of each other, flashes of white and pink. The sound, the groan and moan. The hardness and the wetness, the groping and wanting and needing. We change character before our very eyes.

That was the first time Jack Kerouac was inside of me. He was strong and sure, and I realized now that I would have to actually read his books.

Chapter 4

We never actually slept.

In the early dawn Jack ordered up champagne, orange juice, coffee, poached eggs, oatmeal, smoked bacon, bagels and lox, whatever fascinated him on the room service menu.

I had never been with a man with tattoos before. There were small, subtle Chinese characters on his ankles and wrists, but it was the pair of great, green dragons firing up his back that made me worry about our compatibility. I realized he had been careful with their placement, avoiding the arms, neck, chest, and face, wherever the camera ordinarily went.

"What are you thinking?" he asked like any new lover, his voice as sweet and curious as a teenage boy's.

We were lying in bed, naked and soft, his arm around me. I was thinking two things. I was thinking firstly that I liked how he'd taken me, selfishly in that way that is somehow unselfish, somehow understanding that by taking from me naturally and happily that he was actually giving to me. I decided to tell him the other thing instead.

"I'm thinking of the first novel I can remember finding on our shelves that had sex in it that held my attention. I wish I could tell you the book was *Lolita* or something by Henry Miller. But it was this trashy bestseller called *The Other Side of Midnight* that I just couldn't put down. I was probably twelve years old, and I thought it was the sexiest thing ever. I hid it under my bed so that my father wouldn't know."

"I've never heard of it," he said, rightfully so.

"The late Sidney Sheldon, the seventh best-selling novelist of all time."

"What's your point? That the flesh is as fleeting as an international bestseller?"

"You made me feel trashy and sexy like one of Sidney Sheldon's novels. And I liked the feeling."

Room service knocked. We put on robes and tried to act as if we weren't the whores we had been all night, as if the red-bow-tied waiter from another continent would care, anyway. Jack guessed correctly that his accent was Ethiopian. He busied himself finding room on the table for the many plates on his cart.

"You want me to open the champagne?"

Jack shook his head and gave the waiter a hundred-dollar tip. "That's for having to bear witness to the ending of what is obviously a night of insane debauchery. I hope you and your children and your children's children can forget what your eyes have seen here today."

Jack was every bit the television star, fully aware of his own charisma and ability to take over a scene. The Ethiopian smiled at him with the same awe-filled look that he might give a comet streaking across the sky. Once he was gone, Jack was quick to pop the champagne and to catch the overflow in our glasses.

He touched my glass and said simply, "Skol."

"I could get used to champagne in the morning," I said gaily.

He said way too seriously, "We need to talk."

I immediately jumped to sexual conclusions. "Is this because we didn't use a condom?"

"My sexual health is topper. I hope yours is, too."

"I'm fine, as far as I know."

"I know we should've talked about that beforehand, too. It's my fault, everything unfolded differently than I imagined."

"What is it, Jack?"

"You don't even know my real last name. In this case, it very much matters. Scotty, you better sit down for this."

He filled our glasses again and we both tilted back. "Jack, you're really starting to frighten me."

Jack picked up the manuscript he brought with him. "I wanted to talk to you about this last night. I really didn't figure we would happen this way."

Suddenly, I had a bright flicker of hope. "Is this about me reading your book, is that all this is?" I said trying to be funny. "Of course, Jack. You did the right thing, you slept with me and now I'll give that thing a good thorough read. Sleep your way right to the top of the bestseller lists."

"This is going to feel bad, and that is the last thing I ever wanted. I feel like I've known you all my life. We're very tied together, even though you don't know it. I've always known who you are, my whole life I grew up knowing you. Even if you don't know me from Adam."

"Jack, I don't know who you are right now."

"Your mother was Elsie Dorian."

"Yes, she ran off when I was a three-year-old."

"To California. To make the movie of her book. Her novel—*A Model Life*—is so underrated."

"Did you learn this from the internet, too?"

"My last name is Gregory, don't you see? My father's name is Shane Gregory."

Shane Gregory, the screenwriter. Shane Gregory, who my mother had left us for. Shane Gregory, who was with her at the Hotel Shangri-La when she accidentally overdosed.

He kept talking, which I couldn't understood why he would, "My novel is all about who we are and the river that flows under all of us. I've been writing it since college. It's called *Second Family*. You and Bumby are in it."

All the members of my family were dead. I was too young to remember my mother at all. And my father and I made it a point to never even visit California. But all these years I have always wondered about her and the man who'd destroyed us all. I just slept with the man's son, and I felt nothing but an utter unachievable blankness.

Chapter 5

The Beaux-Arts mansion that was home to Dorian and Cage was as rarified as the rest of my life, its neoclassical edifice occupying a princely piece of Fifth Avenue real estate at the beginning of Central Park, overlooking the zoo, a walkable twenty blocks from where I lived.

If ever we were bought by that phantom media conglomerate of speculation, it would be the first thing they would liquidate. The colossal mansion was built in 1899 by a robber baron who had made his fortune in copper mines, railroads, and Western Union. It seemed right that a publishing company, another relic-sounding enterprise, would occupy the space now and be the next to go.

The building had never really been big enough for our needs, and a percentage of our staff, the troops from publicity and marketing and finance and legal and HR, worked out of the Flatiron Building, on several floors we leased from a larger, rival publisher. Marty and my father liked the idea that we would only share our literary mansion with the legendary editors and writers who understood our old-fashioned, brandy-sipping ways, what they both liked to call the timeless pursuit of literature. Besides the regal dens provided for our top people, my father saw to it that Dorian and Cage always kept available several offices for cherished authors in the throes of madness, which is how they always described any author's current project.

In very real ways our publishing concern was hopelessly out of date. The Big Five, the mad geniuses of mergers and acquisitions, would not know what to do with us. They would gut us like a fish, I supposed. Knife out the firm's bony, old editors and unchecked expense accounts. Cut the head off Marty and me—and put the For Sale signs out in the windows of the mansion—all on Day One.

My father shielded us from so much. He knew the world as it was, and he had no illusions about it, many in his family had perished in the concentration camps, and he made an absolutely deliberate choice to live as we did, sequestered and removed from the insanity that some prefer to call experience, content to stroll our twenty blocks to work and back, all the life anyone really needed, he used to say.

My father was careful. But in the end he fell in love with a Scandinavian model who had somehow written a book as savant-like as Zelda's *Save Me the Waltz*. She was half my father's age but had already packed more in her short life than he could even fill a bucket list with. He was captivated by Elsie's beauty, who wasn't, and in every photo of the two of them I can see his eyes adoring her, while at the same time my mother the model who was so expert at faking it for the camera can't seem to show the same reciprocity.

I didn't know if I was my mother's daughter or my father's daughter today. I had taken such a chance with Jack Kerouac— or should I now say Jack Gregory—which seemed to belie the lonely, risk-adverse life that had come before him. Just as my ever-cautious father had once taken a chance with the young, adventurous model.

I was connected now to my mother in ways that could hardly be imagined. I had slept with her lover's son. What Shakespearian madness. I wondered perversely if Jack's father looked like him, felt like him.

Jack's novel stared back at me from my desk. I didn't dare read his opening sentence.

My corner office held a panoramic view on the park, its greenery like a wide calming ocean, and usually that is where my eyes went. I also had windows overlooking the boutique hotel next door. Often I kept the blinds down because the view depressed me. For some it would've been a voyeur's dream, all those hotel windows with seemingly none of the curtains drawn.

Today I pulled the blinds up. I could clearly see them in their rooms, businessmen choosing ties, toweling off after a shower, businesswomen pinning up their hair, wandering about nude, happy with this small freedom, maids remote-controlling the television. Of course I also witnessed scenes of copulation, silent figures approaching each other with terrible deliberation. I watched men engaged in the usual, going down on faceless women, taking them from behind, sometimes fucking other men. Later I'd see these same men spilling back out onto the street in their wrinkle-free suits, freshly shaved and talced, with their public smiles intact, as if even the most unadulterated of human experience lacked staying power.

Lizza Morris knocked at my door and half let herself in. "Don't forget you have lunch with Dalton Ford today."

Lizza may've been head of publicity, but it also sometimes felt like she did double duty as my executive assistant. She never complained about it. "What's the latest?"

She let herself fully in and closed the door behind her. "I think I'm going to need to take a leave of absence, Scotty. Mara served me with papers this morning. I'm an awful wreck."

It was a day for the lawyers: Stuart would be served with the restraining order and divorce papers when he landed in Frankfurt. It was worth any expense.

"There's something else," she said. "Brace yourself. Gawker has posted someone's photos of you and Jack Kerouac at Blue Bar."

"How bad is it?"

"You're making out with America's newest stud. They'll be

in every New York daily tomorrow. He is very cute, I grant you that."

"I suddenly feel like I'm living in a Sidney Sheldon novel."

Dalton Ford was as famous for his big, bombastic novels as he was for his legendary drinking and gluttonous appetite for life. He was a man's man, a former boxer who had been known to stir up a staid literary gathering with a well-chosen, publicity-charged punch. Then there were Ford's six acrimonious marriages and his many incendiary, short-lived friendships, all played out for the benefit of the press, to boost his rhino-sized image.

Dalton was seventy-eight years old now and none the wiser for having lived so long. He was a paunchy, balding, cauliflower-earred, bulbous-nosed, sloppily-dressed megalosaur whose best feature was a silver beard that was as memorable as Papa Hemingway's. Ten years ago my father had paid Dalton a heavy advance to write his own *Moveable Feast*, a remembrance of his early days and the writers and artists who had befriended him and influenced him, but so far the only writing we had seen was an unwieldy, uneditable few hundred pages of mean-spirited rant against his former and now-dead novel-writing rivals.

Every year it seemed he came looking for a bit more seed money for this fallow field. And every year we treated him to an expensive lunch and wrote another check to his agent. As always he chose the restaurant, this time a sleek Nordic Valhalla that had earned two Michelin stars and which prepared gravlax by the gold ounce.

Of course he'd choose a Scandinavian place; it was as if, after all these years, my mother had decided to haunt me.

We were seated at a conspicuous table in the salmon-hued palace and treated like royalty by the owner, who immediately sent over a bottle of French bubbly and a generous supply of beluga and pickled herring. Waiters hovered like wish fulfillment, refilling glasses and bringing more bread as if being telepathically controlled. Dalton Ford was used to such treatment, of course, and was also beyond noticing the niceties that came with his shambly fame.

"One of my favorite book tours was through Sweden for *American Century*," Dalton said. "All that blond custard, never enjoyed so much ass in my life."

A feminist he was not.

We had barely tapped into the champagne when Dalton asked our waiter to bring a sampling of New Zealand whites.

"Dalton," I said, trying to corral him, "I think your memoir really begins to lift off in the late sixties when you were living in Sagaponack on the pond. I'm thinking especially of the chapter detailing your friendships with James Jones and Capote and Willie Morris, all the carousing at Bobby Van's, the breakup of your first marriage..."

"How'd you like the stuff about old Normie Mailer?"

It smacked of the same cruelty that Hemingway had showed Fitzgerald. The whole comparing penises in the restroom in Paris, just the most awful piece of fiction, with no other witnesses alive to tell it.

"You know," I said, "we saw Norman a lot. And he always got my father's first name wrong. Always called him Merlin, every single time. And when I asked Dad why he never corrected Norman, he just said, 'At least he's consistent, which is more than you can say for most writers.'"

Dalton said, "I banged one of his wives and I can tell you it gave me great feral pleasure."

The restaurant's Norwegian owner insisted on preparing a special off-the-menu meal for Dalton. He started him off with bright red slabs of baby seal, which Dalton wolfed down with relish, proclaiming its taste akin to a rare tuna steak. Then he tried the whale stew, which was sprinkled with lingonberries and which he thought to be chewy and stringy, like horse meat he supposed. Dalton was more pleased with the smoked reindeer, which prompted recollections of a Kenyan safari that yielded barbecued antelope.

His food choices seemed almost as extinct as the novelizing world he had come from.

I said, "We're lucky there's nobody here from Greenpeace."

"What the hell are you eating, Scotty?" he asked, sounding truly miffed. "You need to take chances and to learn to live. It's over before you know it."

Dalton was unhappy that I had refused all entreaties to try his exotic taste treats and that I had instead ordered a simple beet salad to go with my arctic char.

"Why not just get salted cod and boiled potatoes," he said. "For all her wildness, that's what your mother used to prepare for us in those gone years."

Dalton, like many of our authors and friends, always stayed with us when he came to town. Our apartment was a veritable hotel for the literary set until my father died. Dalton lived in Bozeman, Montana now. I didn't know who was putting him up this time, but it made me sad that he hadn't wanted to ask me.

"Dalton, what do you most remember about my mother? You know Dad never talked about her after she left."

"Elsie knew how to have fun. I can't believe you're her daughter because you're such a serious, well-intentioned fool and Elsie just knew how to let loose. She didn't worry about the future, none of us did, and she certainly didn't give a rat's ass about what people thought of her. We never went to sleep in those days. Smoking cigarette after cigarette, glass after glass of whisky and wine. By dawn we would still be up talking books, art, and film, as if any of it matters anymore. We still believed in the Great American Novel then. Our conversation could get mighty heated—I mean, who the hell talks about John Updike anymore?"

"I met the son of the screenwriter she ran off with," I said. "Jack Gregory."

"Did you now?" he said, genuinely curious.

"Somebody took photos of us at the Blue Bar, in a compromising position. Be in the papers tomorrow."

"By God, it will boost book sales," he said, as if I had a fresh novel out.

"I went to bed with him."

"Good for you," Dalton said. "How was he as a lover?"

"He was like Max Farlane in your novel *Take Me Home Now.*"

"Mighty fine," Dalton said. "Good comeuppance for your husband. What a sanctimonious prick. It's why I don't stay with you anymore when I'm in town."

"What did Stuart do?" I asked, now the curious one.

"He tried to get me to join his client list. He came at me pretty hard. He spread some scurrilous stories about Bramble."

Bramble had been Dalton's agent for over fifty years. He was an old-fashioned gentleman who still did business on a handshake. We made it well known to our editors at Dorian and Cage that when Bramble sent over a book to be considered that we would not keep him waiting.

I said, "I filed for divorce today. The apartment is always available to you, Dalton."

I was so used to hearing Dalton's Olympian pronouncements and thinking of him as a self-absorbed bully with a child's attention span that I was surprised to see the old author beginning to choke up.

"What a relief," he said. "Been at the Y. Most of my friends are crippled or dead now."

"I know the feeling," I said. "I'll let Sadie know to expect you tonight. Your usual room will be prepared and waiting."

He suddenly looked revitalized and he called over for a selection of dessert cheeses and a bottle of aquavit. He insisted I join him in his androcentric pursuits and, indeed, I found myself matching him shot for shot. The aquavit was not my kind of drink at all, a harsh, caraway-tinged spirit that I endured with the help of a sweet, caramel-tasting goat cheese.

Dalton lifted the bottle of aquavit to examine the labeling. "Look here," he said with childish delight, "it says they store the aquavit in sherry casks and they put these casks aboard a ship that must cross the equator two times. Says that these long ocean voyages—through all sorts of temperature zones—are what gives the aquavit it's unique flavor."

"The aquavit has been around the world twice," I said wistfully. "It's done more traveling than I have."

"You're just getting started, sister," Dalton said. "Elsie would be proud of you today."

Chapter 6

I took a seat in Dr. Joyce Rock's airy, immaculate waiting room. I was a few minutes early for our weekly appointment. Joyce had made changes to her office in the last year, as her book climbed the bestseller lists. She rid herself of the dark library wing chairs and the shelves of books that had stood heavy on the mandarin rug. Even the percolating fish tank was gone.

The new waiting room was a pearly white modernist sanctuary, Le Corbusier furniture, champagne carpeting, an intolerance to clutter. The only wall hanging was an oversized comic book panel from a Lichtenstein, alight with the face of a beautiful, distressed blond woman, wiping a tear from her cheek.

I thought of what we'd talk about today. She would be interested that I slept with Jack. I had not returned his multiple texts and calls. How would this effect my divorce, she'd want to know.

I worried that I was not being honest with Joyce. I never spoke of my sexual fantasies, which included both men and women and which were increasingly rape focused. I was scared I was drinking too much, too; it was a rare day that I wasn't tippling. We never went there, either. I didn't want Joyce to think poorly of me and it was my tendency to steer our topics to a familiar and trusted litany: my issues with co-dependency, the narcissism within me, my hatred of Stuart, how much I missed my father and brother.

When Joyce opened the door to her office, I was struck again by her own personal transformation. The tortoise-shell eyeglasses and classic tweed outfits were long gone. She no longer pinned her blond hair up in obedience; how her tresses looked sexual and untamed now, even if it was surely the work of a proven stylist. Then there was the yoga body that seemed unencumbered in plain, though surely expensive, black jeans and a turtleneck. Joyce was exactly my age, but the difference was that I had only recently come out of my own sheltered adolescence, where as she had lived life all along.

The inner sanctum was more of the same chrome and leather modernism, Wassily chairs, a Noguchi coffee table and desk, a cold spareness of the mind. The muted, oyster-colored walls were bare except for her diplomas and a poster-size reproduction of the *Times'* bestseller list for the week her book finally arrived.

"I had sex last night with Jack Kerouac, the actor," I said, occupying my usual position on the couch, going right into it. "Did you notice him at Kent's book party?"

Joyce said, "He's impossible not to notice. He's on electronic billboards in Times Square."

"It's been so long since someone has held me." I said, beginning to get teary. "I forgot how much I missed human touch. Just to be caressed by another."

Joyce passed me a box of tissues. "Do you feel like you were ready for this experience?"

"I feel our work has helped me get here. Joyce, I will never be able to thank you enough, because you saved me. If I hadn't met you I might never have gotten to the bottom of all the insanity with Stuart. How awful life would be if he had remained a mystery to me. I wasted so much more time trying to unlock him."

"You did all the hard work, Scotty. You stuck with it, even when it got really difficult."

Little more than a year ago Joyce used a series of therapy techniques on me—age regression, dream work, and guided imagery—which I had joked at the time felt no different than an elective at the Iowa Writers' Workshop, but which loosened swampy matter at the bottom of my unconscious self. What bubbled to the surface were memories that did not shock so much as provide the missing text that made the book of my life start to make sense.

During the period when I was seven and eight years old, a famous and charismatic author who used to stay with us repeatedly molested me. It was actually a great relief to finally unleash the torrent of self-hatred and unworthiness that filled every mysterious chapter of my growing up. I suspect Bumby was also molested by this same man. The fact that he wrote thousand-page tomes that purported to be the final word on such diverse subjects as Female Eros, the Founding Fathers, McCarthyism, and Jackie Kennedy Onassis suggests a certain authorial narcissism that could not be contained to the printed page.

"I still worry that I can't adequately sense danger," I told Joyce. "All my life I've let these kinds of people in, not understanding why I was drawn to them. What if Jack is another one? I can never be sure."

I noticed that Joyce was not taking notes. Always her pen raced over a yellow-lined legal pad, not today, though.

"Scotty, how long have we been together?" she asked.

"A little over two years," I answered.

"I think it's time to break up," she said.

This was not the first time Joyce and I had this conversation, although I could hear the finality in her voice. When I first came up with the idea of Joyce putting together a book on narcissists and borderlines, we both worried that it was a kind of conflict of interest. I chose a suitable literary agent and ghostwriter for the project, but that was the end of it. I made another editor the point of contact from that moment on and steered clear.

"It will be better this way," Joyce said. "You won't lose me. I promise we will stay friends. I will give you a recommendation for a new therapist. You're ready. Look at you, girl. You've left Stuart. The restraining order is in effect. You don't have to worry about communicating with him anymore. You just had sex with one of the most handsome men in the country. I'd say my work is done."

What was left of our hour Joyce spent talking about a new idea she had for a series of novels about borderlines and narcs. She wouldn't actually write it, of course, she'd leave it to me to find the right ghost. She already saw it a little bit like that *Twilight* series about vampires. These narcs and borderlines are constantly looking for a fresh supply of victims. She called these people Receptacles, and the Receptacles only felt alive when they were reflected back in the eyes of the Narcs. Joyce said she was getting ahead of herself but that she had already cast the movie versions of the books in her head.

It was a strange and unsettling way to end our final session.

When I came out of her office, I saw that Dr. Joyce Rock's next appointment was already waiting there, under the Lichtenstein. She was a beautiful, tragic-looking woman. She lifted herself from the couch with great heaviness, like any other doomed woman. I could only wonder what was ailing her. And she could only guess about the demons that swirled in me. We passed without a word, without a second glance. I'm sure we just assumed the worst.

Chapter 7

The Last Columnist was a midtown saloon where Martin Cage and I had been meeting for Monday happy hours ever since Bernie opened the joint way back when with his book advance.

The bar was busy with regulars, but Marty and I caught Bernie's eye and he set about the task of shaking out our gin martinis.

Bernie Sanderson was a former newspaperman who'd once written a fine, sentimental look-back for us called *The Last Columnist*, which detailed the glory days of New York dailies in the sixties and the maverick columnists whose tough-guy faces used to stare back at us from city buses and news trucks. To enter Bernie's bar was to time travel back to that lost Manhattan of Pete Hamill and Jimmy Breslin and other thrice-a-week gunslingers, whose ghostly byline-photos and columns lacquered the walls.

Bernie also had another claim to fame. He had been a cub reporter at *Newsday*, a Long Island daily, when their resident maverick columnist, Mike McGrady, recruited twenty-four other staffers to hatch a novel so downright bad that it couldn't be denied by a reading public that no longer seemed to require of their books believable characters or even believable prose. McGrady's original memo to the staff, which Bernie kept framed behind the bar, said, "There will be an unremitting emphasis on sex. Also, true excellence in writing will be quickly blue-penciled into oblivion."

Bernie happily contributed a chapter to this lark. McGrady's sister-in-law pretended to be the author, who was given the nom de plume Penelope Ashe. Then they slapped a bare-assed woman on the book's cover and called the whole hot mess *Naked Came the Stranger.* Of course it raced up the bestseller lists. For many it was proof of a new low in American literary culture. Which of course was the point of the hoax.

For Bernie it was the pinnacle of his life. The author-pranksters made the covers of national magazines when all was revealed, and these artifacts were proudly displayed along with the framed book jackets from all over the world, a success that somehow translated to places as far removed as Romania and South Korea. The memorabilia in Bernie's bar always made me think that life came down to one or two decisive moments and that the rest was window dressing.

"What's the good word?" Bernie said, bringing us our drinks and one for himself.

"All life is a slow death," Marty said.

"I filed for divorce," I said.

"I'd sell the bar and retire," Bernie said, "but I owe a ton to Uncle Sam."

"I probably got a year left, two at the most," Marty said.

"I got a restraining order against Stuart."

"My kid lost his job again," Bernie said.

"My daughter hasn't had a job in five years," Marty said.

"I still can't grow hair or inches," said Bernie, who was bald and short.

"My psychiatrist left me today," I said.

"Well, I think we have a winner," Bernie said, clinking our glasses. "Cheers."

For some reason this weekly litany of disaster always made all of us laugh and that's how we always started things at the bar. Bernie left to take care of his demanding throng.

"We have to have a serious talk," Marty said. "But first I have something for you."

Marty reached into his leather satchel and with the panache of a magician pulled out a gift-wrapped package. I knew it was a book, and I knew it was probably a very special one. This was not a wild guess on my part because the only presents Marty and I exchanged were first edition novels by writers we mutually admired. Over the last couple of years I had made it my mission to hunt down his hero Saul Bellow's original hardcovers; *The Adventures of Augie March* was already wrapped in my closet awaiting Marty's upcoming birthday, when he would turn eighty and likely enter the final corridor.

Over the last decade Marty had had a series of strokes that required a ghastly amount of speech and physical therapy. Yes, he walked with the help of a cane now and his left side was virtually useless—but this was a victory to all of us.

"I know your birthday is tomorrow," he said, "but I'll never get you alone then. Go on, unwrap it. I want to see your smile."

I did smile as I unwrapped enough of the gold paper to see the title. *A Sport and a Pastime* by James Salter. Originally published in 1967. Doubleday, Garden City. What a tender, sad, erotic, gorgeously modulated dream of a novel it was. I caressed the minty book jacket as if it was a Monet, admiring how different the blue and orange artwork was from the many trade and mass paperback editions that would come later on, which were more sexually conceived.

I gave Marty a hug and a kiss on a grizzled cheek. "It's perfect, I'm so happy for it. You are the best friend ever."

I thought for a second how much I admired not only his taste but that over all the years he was one of the very few males who had never once acted inappropriately with me, not even offering the slyest of come ons.

Marty called down to Bernie for two more martinis. He was not supposed to drink anything but a single glass of red wine on rare occasion, doctor's orders, but Marty flouted that advice as if it wasn't any more serious than a weatherman warning of a possible storm in a ten-day forecast.

Marty said, "Partner, it is time to sell our little publishing concern. I will not be around much longer. I don't want to be one of those cliches that waits to retire and drops dead on the golf course before he can ever really enjoy what's left."

"Marty, you don't even play golf. Publishers and authors are not allowed to retire, you know that. Our work is eternal."

"My mind is made up, Scotty. It will be worse if I die and my percentage in the company goes to Marta and Nat. Then it will be a nightmare to sort out."

Marta and Nat were his middle-age children. Marta lived in Provincetown with her girlfriend, and Marty sent her a monthly allowance. Nat was a software engineer in Mountain View who hadn't made his way home in many years. Marty's wife Ada had died a few years ago after a long, drawn-out cancer. Sadness and a diminished sense of life's possibilities had become the new norm.

Bernie came down to our end of the bar with a new set of martinis. "Great writer," he said, seeing my unwrapped Salter. "Did you read *All That Is?* Magnificent. He published it at age eighty-seven. Kind of gives a guy hope."

The old, the dead, and the dying were all around me. The newspaper business had lost its sparkle and fun and was now just a diminished bottom line. The maverick columnists had saddled up and ridden into the sunset. Publishing was no longer as we once knew it. Novelists were as endangered as poets. And half of Leo's clientele—a Kennedy-era gallery of the solemnly devout— would soon be gone to the other side. The other half, for some unfathomable reason, were the young, chic, and restless who were forsaking their usual aquamarine haunts and bestowing most unwanted of-the-moment status on the bar, as if in their protean slumming they sensed this was the last of something, a mortal ending to the artful lives that had preceded them.

At the Last Columnist veterans of foreign wars and palsy- afflicted widows competed for stools with young women in bullet bras and scowling young men branded in leather. But the juke box suffered from no such split personality. All the songs were from the year 1969 when Leo was a young cub and *Naked Came the Stranger* made its indelible splash.

I knew the juke by heart, we had been here so often. "Everybody's Talkin'" by Harry Nilsson, Glen Campbell's "Galveston," Elvis and "Suspicious Minds," "Sweet Caroline" by Neil Diamond, The Doors's "Touch Me," Sammy Davis Jr. and "I've Gotta Be Me"—at the moment Bob Dylan was singing "Lay, Lady, Lay."

Marty said, "We have an offer from one of the biggies. It's not perfect. We'll have to fold into them. We'll make sure you get your own imprint, Scotty Dorian Books. We'll go over the figures tomorrow. It's a good enough deal when you think about how quickly the world is changing. And you and I and nobody else can take that on."

Maybe it is finally time to let go, I thought. We are working so hard to maintain what once was so easy.

The next song to click on was Johnny Cash's "A Boy Named Sue." I thought for a moment about how many of the artists on the jukebox were still even alive today. Not many. Even Jack Kerouac would be dead before 1969 ended.

Chapter 8

When I arrived home at 1040, Darren gave me a funny little officer's salute and held the door open for me. "Good evening, Miss Dorian. It's good to know Mr. Dalton Ford is back here again with us."

"I'm glad for it too, Darren. Brings back the good old days."

"There was quite a delivery of flowers for you today also," Darren said.

I supposed they were from Jack Kerouac.

"Darren, there's something else," I said. "Mr. Ogden is never to be allowed in the apartment again. Not ever. Not for any reason."

"Your lawyer has already informed us of the situation," he said, not looking too unhappy about it. "I also have a letter that was messengered in for you about an hour ago."

He reached into his Prussian General's uniform and pulled out a missive from my attorney, Leyton Smulders. I tore it open in front of Darren, anxious to know if something had gone wrong today.

> Scotty, just heard from Stuart's attorney. They have asked that we not touch, handle, destroy, remove or store any of Stuart's belongings. They will send someone over from their firm to inventory and vacate said items at a mutually agreeable time. Do not be alarmed, this is not so unusual. I left emails and messages, but I know you often go long periods without checking into our modern world. Cheers, Leyton

"Everything all right?" Darren asked.

"Vacate and remove are good words," I said, considering it.

I got into the mahogany elevator feeling a sense of freedom that seemed only half-remembered, as if after too many years in the valley my world was finally righting itself into peaks again.

Leyton, like Marty, was one of my great protectors, a man to be counted on in the difficult times, which whether you liked it or not were as inevitable as the seasons. It didn't matter how beautifully you managed life's affairs, how perfect your finances and diet, or if you made the most splendid choice of a spouse, sooner or later we were all put to the test. That so many of us could deny such a fundamental and harsh reality was hardly surprising, considering the human need to make a benign and godly sense of our time here. I have always felt that the subtext of every novel ever written is that there must be, how could there not be, a purpose to our lives and the lives that will come after us. No novelist could write a single word if he did not believe that.

Leyton's firm was not only handling my divorce, but he had in fact been handling my father's divorce from my mother at the time of her death. And if Marty and I really let go of the publishing house, I'm sure that Leyton would be one of the attorneys advising us there too, even if that wasn't his specialty.

The apartment overflowed with roses of every color, yellows and whites and reds and blues, vases and vases of them greeting me in every vestibule and hallway. It stunned me and made me feel light and girlish, a feeling that I was unused to, a sweet sense that I meant something to someone. Truthfully, no one had ever done anything like this before for me. I kept pausing to touch and smell the different varieties, and I also looked for a card of some sort.

I paused also when I came to the closed door of Stuart's study. Out of twisted curiosity, and surely I should've just left well enough alone, I decided to enter. I had not ventured in there in quite some time; Stuart had made it very clear to me, as well as to Sadie, that it was strictly off-limits.

Except for one thing it remained unchanged from what I remembered, bookshelves loaded down with Stuart's authors, vintage wood filing cabinets, all anchored by the mammoth, oak rolltop that had once been Leo Gross's writing desk. Stuart also bought Leo's kingly executive chair, a red leather beauty, at the estate auction.

The one thing was actually five things. Parked on a coffee table were five ancient typewriters that I had never seen before. The biggest was an electric IBM Selectric III, its buffed shell a mod orange, that was probably vintage 1970-something. The other four were manuals, whose years of manufacture I couldn't guess at. They were beautiful-looking machines, appearing well oiled and maintained, all of distinctive coloring. I moved in for a closer look, reading their names off their burnished hoods: a sky blue Olympic Traveler, a mint green Hermes Rocket, an oyster white Olympia Splendid, and something called an Erika in a military green.

It was awfully odd. I wondered if Stuart had just suddenly taken up collecting typewriters as a new hobby. Maybe they were the machines of dead authors whom he'd admired.

Stuart had been keeping so many secrets from me that I couldn't even begin to guess. Georgie the private eye had recommended that I just snatch his phone when he wasn't looking; she said people weren't very careful and that it would all be revealed in the text messages and call data. I would never do such a thing, of course. Even though I did catch Stuart going through my own phone one time on the pretense that his was out of juice and he needed to find a number.

The many little drawers and compartments on his rolltop were locked shut. As were the drawers of his filing cabinets. I knew because I tried them all.

I heard voices and laughter coming from the living room, and believing it was Dalton and Sadie I made my way to that end of the apartment. The hearth crackled and sparked with a cheery fire. Dalton Ford and Jack Kerouac, surrounded by the empire of my father's book collection, rose simultaneously from their armchairs to greet me.

"Look who I found in the lobby of the building," Dalton said. "Jack Kerouac, looking more alive than ever. In fact, in life Jack never looked so well."

"Dalton knew Kerouac," Jack said excitedly. "And he's been telling me all these great stories that I've been soaking up."

"I'm glad you're here," I told him, and I was glad in the way that you never knew these things until they are right upon you. "What are we drinking? I want one."

The coffee table held the remains of a half-eaten cheese tray and multiple bottles of my best cabernet, as well as a half-emptied decanter of cognac. Dalton was home at last.

Dalton said, "Let me fetch us another bottle of the old grape. I know where everything is." He had the good sense to wink at me before disappearing into the dining room, where we kept the good stuff.

Jack came over to me and kissed me, and I just let him. His hands felt good on my back as he pulled me in, and he smelled of brandy and cigarettes and that same woodsy cologne he was wearing last night. When we pulled apart, I said, "I didn't know you smoked."

"There's not a lot you do know about me."

"Let me guess you smoke cancer sticks because Jack did too."

"Your mother smoked," he said.

"Let me have one," I said.

Jack took out a pack of American Spirits from his denim shirt pocket and shook out a couple. He lit mine, and then his. It was as easy as that, I was smoking for the first time since college.

"Thank you for the roses," I said, remembering how to blow out rings of smoke. "Did you rob a funeral home?"

"I'm sorry how it ended this morning," he said.

What a bender it had been today. Champagne in the morning, drinking with Dalton at lunch, happy hour with Marty. Where there should have been utter, catastrophic exhaustion there was instead strange elation.

Dalton came in with a pair of freshly uncorked bottles, which felt like another invitation to stay up all night. Dalton had given up smoking years ago, too, but he joined us for a cigarette without hesitation.

"What should we drink to?" Dalton asked, after filling our goblets with wine. "I know," he said. "Good riddance to that fucking husband of yours."

"I haven't had such fun in years," I said. "We need music."

I showed Jack the Jurassic stereo system and asked him to pick out some records. Soon my home was filling up with sweet, sweet sounds that hadn't been heard in many years. To hear Marvin Gaye's gorgeous voice after so long, to remember so many evenings with my father and his friends, brought me to the edge of tears. Sadie came in to check on us, and it felt no different than if we had been teenagers engaged in a secret party and been found out by somebody's mom.

I asked Sadie to join us, and soon she was enjoying wine and taking turns dancing with Dalton and Jack. The records kept changing, we never let the fire burn down, we kept bringing new bottles out, and somewhere into it Jack asked Dalton to read for us. I went to the shelves and found my favorite book of his. I knew just where it was, even though I hadn't read it in many years. It was published in 1975, half a lifetime ago for Dalton, and I realized that he had written it at the exact same age as I was now. He won the Pulitzer for it, but that's not what made it good.

Inside there was a personal inscription to my father: "Thank you for providing loving sanctuary, as always." *Shadow of Me* was a searingly honest account of Dalton's crack-up and the years of electro-shock that came after. I hadn't heard Dalton read in some while, and I had truly forgotten not just how profound a writer he'd once been but how powerfully he could hold you. The intimacy with the reader, the absolute insanity of his life and all of our lives, a craziness in the mirror that he never flinched from. Why, Dalton truly deserved his prizes and fame. He did what few could do: he let us look inside. All the bluster would come later.

I'm not sure if I was ever happier than this night. To sit on the couch with Jack's arm around me listening to Dalton's powerful, sonorous voice, all of it bringing me back to the cherished life we had constructed here in these rooms, so rich with purpose that the thought never occurred to us that it could end. Private readings by extraordinary authors were just a part of growing up for us. We never took it for granted, but it was commonplace enough that my father and I devised a way to communicate when an author was going on for too long or just plain boring us. He tapped his pipe twice and that was the signal for me to stand up and make some excuse about an early morning the next day.

I didn't have to know where any of this was yet going. But hearing Dalton tell his truth made me want to be that way with Jack. If we were going to do this I wanted to know him and I wanted him to know me. I was just drunk enough to believe this might be possible. I knew one thing for sure, though, and that was that the night would end in my bedroom with Jack on top of me.

Chapter 9

It was late in the morning the first time I woke up. Jack wished me a happy birthday, I gather that's on the internet, too, and then he went down on me. He was such a nimble lover that I had to wonder how many women he had been with. He was famous and in demand and I harbored no illusions. I did not expect to be able to keep Jack. I enjoyed myself, and with each wanton fuck I felt a great and necessary erasing of Stuart.

In the remains of the night I learned some more about Jack. He maintained an apartment on the Upper West Side and also kept a place in Los Angeles. He'd studied acting at the Yale Drama School. He had a twin sister. It took his father ten years to get over my mother and to be able to love again. The broken pieces that make a life.

I thought you'd want to know that we went without protection again. There were no condoms in the apartment, and besides I had already dispensed with caution the previous night. I had not been able to conceive with Stuart in the year we tried and I worried less about pregnancy than about an STD, which I really didn't worry about either because I had already made my decision and why second guess what's been done, which felt like a brave new philosophy for me.

Jack would not let me reciprocate his sexual gift. He said the day belonged to me. With that I retreated back into a languorous sleep. When I woke again it was early afternoon, to judge by the lush light coming through my windows. The phone confirmed it, 1:14. I had never done anything like this before on a weekday; I arrived most days at the office promptly by ten.

I put on a robe and wandered out into the hallway to search for Jack. Jazzy music was pulsing from the big room. I also heard the distinct sound of typing. Whoever was typing was typing very fast, to hear the clacking and the constant ding and swipe of the carriage. It turned out to be Dalton, who had set himself up in a corner of the cavernous living room, making use of an extremely rare antique writing desk that had been my father's. That's not what concerned me. It was that Dalton was tapping out his manuscript with the sky blue Olympic Traveler that had been in Stuart's study. A pile of pages fluttered beside him, ruffled by the breezes coming off the park. I was glad for the sight of Dalton working again, if a bit worried about the use of the typewriter.

Dalton turned to me looking so cheery-eyed that I couldn't possibly be mad. He said, "Come, sit, read. This book is writing itself now. Last night was a tonic for me. What a joy to be knocking it out again. And with Mr. Charlie Parker on the hi-fi, no less. What could be finer?"

He handed me his pages, maybe twenty in all, which hardly seemed possible, and I planted myself in a cozy corner of my favorite couch. I braced myself, even a single paragraph will reveal a book's genealogy and destiny. Jack had left a pack of his cigarettes out on one of the coffee tables, and I helped myself to one and once suitably fortified I began to read. Dalton's first sentences were like the music, punchy, up-tempo, landing in unexpected places.

"I had a Traveler once myself," Dalton said at the typewriter. "Indestructible. Fine, fine machine."

"I'm glad you located it," I said, thinking to hell with Stuart. "I'm surprised you were able to find the paper to go along with it."

"About that," he said sheepishly. "I looked everywhere, and I was mad on a mission. The thing of it is, kiddo, I may have broken a lock or two on those old filing cabinets. Found what I was looking for. Heaps of blank paper in there."

The paper seemed old and expensive, with its watermark and thick fibrous quality. Dalton had struck the keys hard and his letters weighed into the paper like braille. He was doing just what I had hoped, returning to Sagaponack but this time with heart and generosity towards his old literary comrades. It was very, very good, and it was almost great.

"I love it," I said to Dalton. "I'm over the moon for it. Keep going, don't stop, you are so on a roll."

Jack came in with coffee in a French press and a tray of Bloody Marys.

"Brunch will be out shortly," he announced. "Sadie and I have prepared your favorites."

I forsook the coffee for the Bloody Mary. Jack made a stingingly strong drink, heavy on the vodka, the Worcestershire and horseradish.

Dalton was delighted with it. "Better than the one at the King Cole Bar. Vonnegut and I holed up there one year doing the hard detective work of trying to ascertain their exact recipe."

"Thought Kurt had been a scotch and soda drinker."

"All I remember was smoking those awful Pall Malls with him, both of us coming out of torporific marriages. He wrote the one book, though, that's all you have to do."

I knew Dalton was referring to *Slaughterhouse-Five*. I said the signature line, "So it goes."

"Come to think of it, maybe he just wrote the one sentence."

"That's not fair," I said. "He wrote over a dozen books. Dalton, you and your memoir are much better when you show your sweet sentimental side."

"This memoir is fast becoming fiction."

Soon we were gorging on popovers and eggs Benedict and slabs of Canadian bacon. There were jams and cheeses and all the goodies. I believe it was when we were on our third or fourth round of Bloody Marys that Jack took out a baggie of pot and a pipe and said we should all get stoned. I remember thinking it was an absolutely sensational and inspired idea at the time. Dalton concurred, though Sadie abstained.

We had to be at the office by four. It was a tradition to have my editors and authors in for cake and champagne on my birthday.

Jack and I took a shower together. We sang "Yellow Submarine" and "Hey Jude" at the top of our lungs while we soaped up. Jack suggested we cut a record together, and for me it wasn't clear if he was being funny or not.

My father had been about Jack's size, and we went into his bedroom, which still held all of his things in place. If you want to be Freudian about it that is certainly your right, but Freud is a chauvinistic, discounted author who thought female sexual desire was hysteria. I picked out a fresh shirt for Jack and a jacket that I thought he'd look smashing in.

"Hilditch and Key," Jack said with a big, phony Brit accent, holding up the fancy shirt with barrel cuffs. "Exquisite, my dear. It will be a charming addition to my wardrobe of denim and khaki."

He looked like a young, hot English Lord, and we made love again, think what you will, this time on my father's bed.

Soon after Jack called for his driver and car, which seemed to arrive in mere minutes, or at least everything felt that way. Jack, Dalton, Sadie, and I got into the Range Rover like it was a magic carpet ride and we floated above the city.

I said, "Did any of you ever actually read Fitzgerald's second novel, *The Beautiful and Damned?*"

Dalton said, "F. Scott's powers weren't yet mature enough to power that book."

"Exactly. But later he would tell Zelda that it was the truest book he ever wrote. Drink after drink, party after party. I feel like I'm living in that novel."

Jack did that annoying thing people do now which is to tap out a note on his iPhone to remind himself to read *The Beautiful and Damned*.

"While you're at it, you might as well make a note to purchase the complete works of John Cheever and Richard Yates and Raymond Carver. That way we will be more compatible."

"That's quite a bitchy thing to say," Dalton said in Jack's defense.

"I must be quite high," I said. "That was surprisingly ungenerous of me."

"I actually have read Carver," poor, dear Jack said. "Scotty, when was the last time you smoked?"

"Iowa, the year of our lord 2001, which was also a space odyssey."

We arrived an hour late to my party, and when we walked into the marbled, columned lobby of Dorian and Cage we were greeted by the odd applause of editors and guests who were probably becoming doubtful that we'd show at all. Helium balloons floated up the commanding stairway to the second floor of the mansion, clustering like the guests on the perimeter hallway that led to the office suites.

Dalton and Jack fetched glasses of rose champagne for us, my favorite, and I began to make the rounds. These parties always reminded me of a high school dance, the same kind of savage cliques, even if people hold more noble estimations of us in the literary world.

Sully Sullivan, an editor as ancient as the Dead Sea Scrolls, held court with the East Hampton crowd. Sully's novelists had had their great successes in the seventies and eighties and for the most part they were no longer, really writing, although no one would actually admit this salient truth. All of their current projects were like Dalton's, years in the making, to be discussed over gin and tonics at dinner parties. All were encouraged to nod and look interested. Talk of reissued novels and teaching seminars at the Ivys was the normal chit and chat. Releasing their letters and their journals would be the final step on life's conveyor belt.

Sully's novelists would have little to do with the younger set clumping around Nicki Alvarez, a senior editor who belying her title was fresh out of grad school. Nicki, who favored button-down shirts and Dunhill cigarettes, was brought into the house so that in our dotage we didn't miss out on publishing whole genres entirely. Nicki brought in graphic novels and LGBT pulp fiction and hardcore chick lit and other fascinations that left some of our mummified staff utterly mystified.

We steered clear of cookbooks, travelogues, science fiction, fantasy, young adult, and children's literature. But we were heavy on Brit lit and Jewish lit and translations of South American authors. We also had a strong footing in biographies and literary memoir. Hendricks, a tall, old reed in Harris tweed, stood talking to Meyer Havens, the author of what was now approaching eight volumes on RFK with no end in sight—I believe the last one had only propelled us forward to the year 1964— except for his own grave.

Listening politely to their shop talk was Leyton Smulders, who as a lawyer knew better than to offer opinions. Leyton, an invisible man in pinstripes, nodded and kept a permanent half smile on his strategic face. Besides representing my family in legal matters for forty years, Leyton was also an author. He had written a powerfully instructive autobiography, that had been starred by *Publisher's Weekly* and widely praised elsewhere, detailing his rise through the ranks as a black attorney to head one of the top white-shoe firms in Manhattan.

"Gentlemen," I said in greeting.

I felt slightly unsteady on my feet. Fortunately I never really had to speak to my editors and authors. It was my job to listen to them. They always wanted something. Deadline extensions, better advance money, better publicity, yada yada yada.

"There's a photo of you and Jack Kerouac canoodling in the *Daily News*," Hendricks said quite sourly. "I'll admit I was never much of a fan of Kerouac's work. Although I know some people who left their jobs and marriages because of that *On the Road* horseshit. All that imagined wanderlust. As for Kerouac he hasn't written a word in years as far as I know."

Hendricks was an actual editor who not only made excellent acquisitions but took the time to befriend his authors. He was nicknamed the Crop Duster oddly enough for his ability to spray clouds of lucid editorial comment over the lush, green fields of prose his writers turned in. But lately the Crop Duster had seemed strangely less lucid.

Meyer said, "Have you ever seen that classic photo of Jacqueline Kennedy reading *Dharma Bums* on Air Force One? What a collision of worlds."

Lizza Morris stepped into the conversation. "Gore Vidal said in his memoirs that he slept with Jack Kerouac at the Chelsea Hotel."

"Jack's here today," I said, pointing him out. "And I slept with him an hour ago."

Leyton raised an eyebrow of concern.

"So the rich get richer," Lizza said before she had the sense to retract it. "Sorry, Scotty. I haven't been myself since Mara left. Other people's happiness seems to grate."

Meyer said, "I think it was Vidal who also said, 'Every time a friend succeeds, I die a little.'"

Jack was still over by the bar, having not made much movement, his way blocked by a phalanx of admirers looking to have their existence confirmed by a celebrity.

"I never really imagined you'd be interested in that type of writer," Hendricks said, sounding slightly loopy. "Why, he's not for you, can't you see that? You've always yearned for a certain structure in your life. Kerouac doesn't edit his work. It's all free-form garbage. Everything is in the editing, you know that, Scotty."

"I believe I read somewhere that Kerouac and Ginsberg gave each other blowjobs," Lizza said, still not herself.

I quickly excused myself, wondering if Hendricks was in the early phases of dementia and if Lizza had any sense left at all. Of course I was as insane as everyone else, dropping that bit about sleeping with Jack. I seemed only one mad step away from listing for everyone the positions we were doing it in, all that Philip Roth shamelessness.

Georgie Guns, vamped up in a shimmery gold swathe that private investigator Nicoal Angel might've worn in her series opener *Vegas Nights*, cornered me next. "I have some information on Stuart."

"Shouldn't we talk privately?"

"This will just take a second," she said, guzzling back champagne.

Now I should tell you that I hired Georgie to look into Stuart for me. I wasn't going to steal his phone or break into his filing cabinets as Dalton had done. The worst you could accuse me of was a distinct lack of boundaries; one author was a shrink, another did detective work for me, and the man I was screwing was a Beat author who'd been dead for decades.

"He and Kent are romantically involved," she said. "They're in Germany together. Same hotel room, I'm sure using the same toothbrush."

I wasn't shocked, I didn't discount it, and I was just glad for this information that matched up with my suspicions. I sensed always that Stuart was unfaithful. I was made crazy by living with a pathological liar who challenged my sense of the real at every mundane turn. If the day was sunny, he could convince me it was gray and overcast with a chance of rain.

It is hard, I imagine, to believe in this nightmare unless you've experienced it. And even harder to understand unless you've actually worked through it with a trained therapist. The handsome, charming man you think you once loved is in reality a serial narcissist always on the prowl for new targets and supply. Nothing prepares you for such a thing. Our greatest writers, who are so adept at capturing voices and finding the humanity in others, stretch with great difficulty to capture the mind of a sociopath. For the sociopath has no inner voice of his own.

I knew Kent was in the idealization phase of Stuart's obsession.

Kent was being wooed and indulged. Stuart was gathering as much information on Kent as he could in this vulnerable, intimate early phase of the relationship. The moments of hideous devaluation would only come later.

"Kent's also off the wagon again, sucking back those Wild Turkey shots," Georgie said. "I've also discovered that there's some bad blood between Susan Ogden and Kent. Do you know anything about that, Scotty? Was Stuart ever romantically involved with his business partner? As either a man or a woman?"

Before I could consider it further, Carlo Bassi, with the help of his bodyguards, wheeled in a towering birthday cake that had been sculpted in the shape of our publishing mansion.

"Made special by the best bakery in Queens," I could hear Carlo saying. I could only hope that nobody had been whacked in the process of baking it.

The candles were lit, and I was called over. Marty came over to join me as the mob began singing a hearty happy birthday. I worried in that moment of group song that we would have to sell the house and many here would soon be out of work.

I blew out the thirty-nine candles, and I made my wish. I wished that Dorian and Cage could go on and on forever and ever.

"Speech, speech!" Dalton Ford cried out.

I said, "You know I always wish for the same thing. World peace and an end to deconstructionist literary theory. Oh, and of course to dominate the bestseller lists in the year ahead."

That's all I had to do before wobbling off to gather another glass of champagne.

The next thing I knew a man in a tuxedo approached me, "Are you Ms. Scotty Dorian?" Then he said, "Consider yourself served," as he handed me a package of legal papers.

"Why are you in a tuxedo?" I strangely thought to ask.

"People don't stop me from entering buildings when I wear the tux," he said.

I started scanning the first page of the clipped papers and I was called the defendant and Stuart was the plaintiff and he was suing me for all sorts of insanity, for fraud, unjust enrichment, I couldn't even begin to fathom what was going on, and the next thing I knew Georgie and Joyce and Carlo and Jack and Sadie and Marty and Leyton and Dalton were all surrounding me and asking if I was okay. I realized only then that I was sobbing.

Joyce and Leyton accompanied me to my office. Jack came too. He was resourceful enough to heist a bottle of champagne along the way. Leyton perused the lawsuit as Jack filled my coffee mug with bubbly.

"It looks ugly," Leyton finally said. "Stuart's going around the prenup. He's claiming that you and your father and Dorian and Cage prospered because of his savvy business advice and acumen during the marriage. This could take years to sort out."

"Oh my God," I cried. "I'll never be rid of him."

"We'll win in the end," Leyton determined.

"I can't go through any more of him continuing to be in my life."

"Remember, this is not about you or money," Joyce said. "It's his need for control and engagement. Stuart doesn't feel alive unless he's engaging you. He had the lawsuit delivered at your party to make sure you feel his grasp."

"You see," I said, crumbling. "He'll never go away."

"Fuck him," Jack said. "We'll kill this freak."

Yes, Jack, kill him. Make it hurt.

"I mean, legally speaking and all."

Oh, is that all?

"And we're not going to let this ruin your birthday, Scotty. I've got an idea where to go next."

"Jack, as long as it's not a gun shop," Joyce said.

"Don't you worry, Scotty," Leyton said, "We'll counter sue for domestic abuse and enslavement. We have serious documentation— Joyce here will testify, there's the restraining order—that you are afraid of this man and that you've been traumatized by him. We will destroy his reputation—"

"Yes, narcissists worry about how they are perceived in public," Joyce said.

I think it was here, not in the way of a passing cloud or an angry flash of lightning but in the way of a pure blue sky on a forever day, that I started to really consider how I would contract a hit on Stuart's life.

Chapter 10

Carlo Bassi's Escalade followed Jack's Range Rover as our group descended on the Minetta Tavern for my birthday dinner. We had not bothered to call ahead. The well-heeled and fashionable clustered on the sidewalk, looking eternally antsy, waiting their turn to be crossed off the list, all of them on their cell phone-connected earpieces, letting their friends know up-to-the-minute updates on the length of their internment, appearing to all the world like a group of insane city people all talking to themselves at once. Once inside they will send photos of their hamburgers to these same patient friends.

Small things like reservations didn't particularly matter when you were with Jack Kerouac and a retired mafia kingpin. The bouncer parted his velvet ropes at once, as if his very life was at risk. A hostess led us into a solid wave of noise: loud, self-satisfied voices and the clanging cutlery of moneyed carnivores. The dining room glowed old-time New York red with its crimson banquettes, checkered tile, and tin ceiling. The walls reflected back the caricatures of boxers, politicians, and socialites who were famous once but unrecognizable to most of us today.

A table was procured for our party of six so quickly that I was left to wonder if the previous occupants had just been escorted out at gunpoint and shot in an alley. I knew exactly why Jack brought us to Minetta. It had a rich, sodden literary history. Opened in 1937 the tavern had entertained generations of the writerly famous, Hemingway and Dos Passos, Ezra Pound and E.E. Cummings, and of course the Beats, Gregory Corso and Ginsberg and Jack Jack Jack Kerouac.

I sat between Marty and Jack, feeling warmly, contentedly protected. Georgie Guns looked just as happy on the other side of the table between Dalton and Carlo.

Dalton, at Carlo's unnecessary prompting, took charge of ordering for us. Soon the wait staff was bringing us before-dinner cocktails, in this case Sidecars, an old favorite of Dalton's. He ordered like Jack, without regard for price and portions, whatever caught his fancy. Soon there were huge platters of foie gras and carpaccio and stuffed calimari and lobster salad being placed before us. Dalton never hesitated and selected fat steaks and blackened veal chops and roasted chickens for our main courses. Nor did he neglect the side dishes, so sure was he that we would need those extra bowls of pommes frites and potatoes Anna. I only worried when Dalton, scrutinizing the wine list, began to speak his perfect French to order five bottles of a burgundy that could not have gone for less than three hundred dollars a pop.

Dalton told the wine steward, "That ought to do us for now. But please check back in the very near future. I noted some other delightful prospects."

"I like this guy," Carlo said about Dalton. "A real fuckin' writer."

"He's totally cute," Georgie actually said about the Pulitzer and National Book Award-winning author.

My Jack started talking about the strange episode involving Kerouac's college friend Lucien Carr. I hadn't heard the story since my studies at Harvard. Carr had murdered a man named David Kammerer. And Kerouac and William Burroughs helped hide evidence of the murder and were arrested as material witnesses.

"Lucien took Kammerer here to the Minetta for lunch shortly before he killed him," Jack said, excited to be in a room lit with dark history.

"Big story in its day," Dalton said. "Newspapers loved its whiff of homosexuality, so taboo back then. Lucien was being stalked by Kammerer for sex, it was said."

"How did he kill the guy?" Carlo asked with professional interest.

"Stabbed him, tied him up with his belt and loaded his clothes with rocks," Jack said. "Then sank the body in the Hudson."

"Not bad for an amateur," Carlo said.

Jack said, "We're putting it in my show using flashbacks."

I'd nearly forgotten how messy, violent, and sordid the lives of the Beats had been. William Burroughs made part of his literary reputation by shooting his lover, Joan Vollner, another in their close inner circle. Burroughs never did any time for it, suspended sentence for involuntary manslaughter.

I looked over at Carlo Bassi, and I knew I would soon be asking him to do something that I hoped wouldn't also become part of the dark lore of the Minetta Tavern.

Jack nudged me. "Take these," he said. "You're starting to doze off."

"Was I?" I said, unsure if that was true or not.

Jack gave me a couple of pills, and I just swallowed them with the wine.

"Don't you want to know what they are?" he asked.

"I trust you."

"Bennies. You'll get a second life, you'll see."

Not long after taking the pills I started to be able to alertly follow things again. Carlo was telling Jack that his novel was under option at Paramount and that the assigned screenwriting team had just finished the first draft. The timing was good, Jack's show was going on hiatus in a few months, and Jack's agent had blacked out time to make a picture. Dalton and Georgie were making each other laugh hysterically by telling awful dirty jokes.

"What do you call a bad blowjob?" Dalton asked.

"I have no idea," Georgie said.

"You call it fantastic!" Dalton said, exploding in laughter.

Marty had been unusually quiet for most of the evening. But as the dessert soufflés arrived, along with bottles of a very old tawny port that Dalton insisted on, he brought me into focus and said, "My dear, tell me about your all-time favorite birthday."

"You know my favorite birthday," I said, touched and glad that he would bring it up.

"How old were you?" Marty asked, happy to be on this path.

"I turned twelve that year."

"What a wonderful year that was. All of us were alive, all of us were together. Indulge an old man and tell it to me again."

"I had just read *The Catcher in the Rye*, and I was in love with Holden Caulfield. And you and Dad decided to surprise me by taking me on a picnic to Cornish, New Hampshire to meet the great man."

Marty said. "We all listened to *Catcher* being read again on the tape cassette in your father's Saab. Do you remember? It was a long, four-hour-plus ride but with the tape on it passed easily. What you probably didn't know, Scotty, is that Salinger never relinquished the audio rights and that the only way one could get their hands on that tape was by being legally blind. Your father found a way, though. He would've done anything for your happiness."

"It was a sunny, magical day," I said, calling it back to me. "I will cherish it always. I remember coming up that dusty driveway, in the middle of nowhere. I don't know how you knew the directions."

"Your father again."

"You both egged me on and pushed me towards the steps up to his house. And I made that lonely walk to the screen door by myself. You stayed by the car and watched me. And I knocked, and my heart was pounding like crazy. And I knew right away it was Mr. Salinger when he came to the door."

"What did you say to him, Scotty? Keep indulging an old man."

"I told Mr. Salinger that he was a great man who had written a great book, I said, 'We drove all the way up from New York City to tell you that. We know you don't talk to strangers. And we won't bother you anymore. We will go back to the city now, but please keep up the good work.'"

"What did the great man say to that?"

I was not sure anymore what Salinger actually said. The story has shifted shape and repeated itself so many times that I am no longer sure it actually happened this way, but I said what I always said, because it had always pleased Marty and my dad so much, "Mr. Salinger said to me, 'You seem like a nice girl. Come back in ten years.'"

Marty laughed as he always did at this telling, to the point of tears. "Come back in ten years," he repeated.

He reached for the bottle of port closest to us and filled our tulip glasses.

"To that rarest of things," he said, clinking me. "A great novel."

Those were the last words I ever heard Martin Cage utter. A moment later he clutched at my hand and looked at me with all the sudden pain in the world and collapsed right then and there to the floor.

Chapter 11

The funeral service was held at the Frank E. Campbell Funeral Chapel at East Eighty-First Street. I had been to Campbell's many times before. If you reached the heights in this city, odds were high that you would someday make a visit here, one way or the other, as a mourner or as an occupant in a pearl-toned casket.

The services for Norman Mailer, Dominick Dunne, and Tennessee Williams had all taken place here. As well as for Lannigan Sinclair, who was put in the ground two days ago. And in this sepulchral brownstone, more to any point, is where I said goodbye to my own father and brother. For Bumby we were glad for Campbell's well-earned reputation for security and discretion, since there had been much vulgar interest in his circumstances.

Someday they would be gathering here to say goodbye to me. I wasn't sure there'd be much to say, frankly. Funerals are always as much about grieving for ourselves and our own-to-come, inevitable passing from the face of the earth as they are for the dearly departed.

Lizza handled the arrangements today, and things appeared to be going as planned. As the chapel filled with mourners, a pianist and a trumpeter played soulful Chet Baker songs that Marty had particularly liked. I sat in the front row with Marty's son and daughter, along with Dalton who had agreed to give the main eulogy. I was also expected to say a few words and introduce Dalton.

The turnout was large, Marty had been beloved. The senior editors from our house were all here, of course. I had closed Dorian and Cage for a week of mourning. Editors from rival houses were here also, as well as a colony of literary agents. Renowned authors from all over the country and the world had flown in, even some like Martin Amis and Salman Rushdie who were not published by us.

I felt the same as I did when we buried my father. I could not grip that my friend's life was over, and I felt along with the stabbing sadness a feeling of absolute wonder—how it happens that a whole and multifarious human life, the one hundred thousand things we touch and love and put our name to, ends stuffed in a box.

I contemplated Marty's long trajectory. After he graduated from Columbia he set himself up in a railroad flat on the Lower East Side. He unhinged a door and placed it on stolen sawhorses. Now he had a desk for his Royal typewriter. And he set out on his long-awaited journey of writing a brilliant and comic novel about his loony Jewish family and their schizoid placement in the American dream, a real Philip Roth number, as he ruefully described it, perhaps sad that someone so gifted had explored the same territory so thoroughly.

What happened to Marty was not so very unusual, involving the pregnant girlfriend and the oh so predictable ways of the world. The novel, something called *Nana's Revenge*, having galloped to page 247, was put on ice for a short while, until Marty could get on his feet financially, and of course it remained in this cryogenic state for the next five decades. It was a strangeness that he kept coming back to, especially in the reflection of a drinking glass, how the book would briefly come alive for him, as if it had been released from its amber, full of warm mystery and glow, and he would once again vow to get to it soon. Every August, during those weeks of hammock swaying on Martha's Vineyard, Marty would procrastinate to the point of paralysis. He finally gave up altogether one summer not so long ago, making permanent the forlorn recitation of missed opportunity and lost glory that is the province of every man.

Now the country has always been bursting at the seams with closet dreamers who will bore you senseless with the potboilers gathering dust in attic boxes, just as the college English departments across the land have always been up to their eyeballs with Chaucerian scholars who think they can writer wonderful modern novels with the biting dialogue of a Steinbeck or a David Foster Wallace. The world will always be full of thwarted dreamers and their rather ordinary dreams.

I realized how glad I was that Marty's dream to finish his novel went incomplete and dark. He did so much more as a publisher than he could ever understand to do as a novelist. He guided into the world thousands of wonderful novels. And started the careers of so many worthy talents that might have gone unseen if it weren't for his sharp sensibilities.

That was it, that was what I would tell the mourners in the chapel. I had been looking for it, and there it was, the little story I could tell. I got up to the lectern and I looked out at the sea of dark-suited men and women, realizing that I had been up here in this exact place multiple times before and that there seemed no end in sight. When you are in your twenties and early thirties you go to the weddings of friends, and there seems to be one every other weekend, and then you hit middle age and the weddings for the most part cease and something new and terrible takes its place.

"Many of us were here three years ago for my father's service," I began. "I gave a eulogy then. My words about Dad brought some laughs and some tears. After I finished I sat back down next to Marty. And Marty, who never stopped editing, whispered to me, 'Nice job. Except when it's time to do my eulogy I don't want you to punctuate it with so many laughs. Go heavier on the dramatic elements of my life.'

"Of course Marty was like a second father to me..."

A man stood up in the very back of the chapel. I think I felt it in my marrow before I could even make him out— it was

Stuart. The sicko actually took his sweet time to study me before sitting back down. So much for restraining orders. As unnerved as I was, I knew he could not harm me in here. He was sending me a message, though, that no place would ever be safe enough. Somehow I plowed on. I told my story about Marty's unfinished manuscript and why we were all so lucky for that and then I introduced Dalton. I knew Dalton had loved Marty. I knew it just by the dignity and care with which he had dressed today; he'd trimmed his beard and bought an expensive dark navy suit.

"Martin Cage was a great friend and a great human being," Dalton said with strength. "Marty's passing is the passing of all that we ever held dear. We are all dying out like the books we once believed in. Our time has come—and it, and we, shall not pass this way again. Death is everywhere in our little world, every one of us like an autumn leaf quivering in the wind, clinging to our last breath of summer..."

It was difficult to listen, knowing Stuart was here. I would not be able to do anything about the situation until the service ended.

Dalton went on too long, hammering in the metaphoric nails, turning Marty's death into the death of generations who had once held books to be sacred, before turning it back to a personal sphere. He told a story of the time Marty came down to Key West because Dalton was months overdue on a novel. Marty discovered Dalton and Hunter S. Thompson crashing on some patron's yacht—a fine vessel that had been utterly befouled by their drinking, whoring, and drug-fueled rampages. Marty was flabbergasted by the wreckage, but Hunter and Dalton assured him that it would be all right, that they had hatched a genius plan. Marty listened in horror as the lunatic authors proposed a propane-tank explosion and collecting insurance money, as if real-life felonies were no more than the notes and outline of a yet unwritten chapter.

As Dalton recounted how Marty brought in a shipyard crew to make repairs, and how he somehow got both Hunter and Dalton back on the road to semi-sanity, I became more conscious of Marty's daughter and son next to me. Marta and Nat did not inherit their father's love for all of this strangeness, and they seemed to shift uncomfortably in their seats listening to Dalton. I knew without question that the estate would demand a sale of Mary's assets and that our publishing house would be dead and history, too.

After the service was over, the sorrowful and ashen-faced got up slowly from their seats, thick with the godawful knowing of what was in store for all of us. There was no sign of Stuart. I could not have imagined it, it just wasn't possible. I wasn't sure if anyone else had taken note of his presence, and knowing Stuart he was extremely careful with his entrance and his exit. He probably had an alibi besides, placing him in some other place at the same time. It would only make me look loopy and unbalanced to report it, probably what he wanted me to do, some odd advantage to him there in this game of gaslighting that he never tired of playing.

Once outside, in the cool autumn air, the mourners were soon talking among themselves, their previously contained voices rising like so much freed music. Photographers jockeyed for position on the sidewalk, with their bazooka cameras, rapid-fire clicking and shooting America's literary elite. The funny thing is, authors are so different from movie stars that for the most part they paused and acquiesced to the paparazzi's demands, the general feeling always being anything to boost book sales.

Lizza came over to say that everything was set for the wake at The Last Columnist. I had bought out the bar for the day, as Marty had wanted and had let me know on many occasion.

"Life is so cruel," Lizza said. "I really do understand why Virginia Woolf just waded out into the river."

"Marty loved his life," I felt compelled to say.

"Well, I don't love mine," she said.

Before I could respond to Lizza, Sully Sullivan approached to let me know he liked what I said at the service. I asked if he would be joining us for drinks.

"Sorry, Scotty," he said. "I've got another funeral to attend. When you get to my age these doubleheaders are not so uncommon."

I watched Sully trudge away, this dignified elderly gentleman in a homburg hat, this pallbearer in life's wintry parade. I knew there'd be a day not too far in the future when we'd gather at Campbell's to say goodbye to Sully and I would be asked once again to take the lectern and in some small way make sense of a whole and multifarious life that was simply gone, deleted with as much subtlety as hitting a backspace key.

Jack found me. He was freshly shaved and in a proper dark suit, and he must have sensed I needed him now. He came over and put his arm around me, and I started to cry, finally, for Marty, for all of us.

Chapter 12

Bernie greeted our guests at the door of his saloon. Bernie, who I'd never seen in anything fancier than a checked sports coat, spiffed himself up in a suit that seemed wholly purchased for funerals. It was a suit that had the sheen of frequent dry-cleanings, which made me sad, thinking about the average age of his clientele.

Bernie hugged me and sobbed out, "Marty was the salt of the earth. They don't make them any better."

"He loved coming here, Bernie," I said, Jack standing beside me, such a crazy comfort. "This was always a bright spot in our week."

"You know he personally lent me money back in the day when I was working to finish the book. No lectures, no anything, just a check. He said, 'Forget about it.' Who does that? I'll tell you who does that—nobody, except Marty Cage."

I could hear the raucous laughter coming from inside The Last Columnist as the authors and editors partook in the free booze and began to tell the stories, which were inevitably funny, of the daily struggles of any writerly life. Marty had helped a lot of them out of jams, and he never made a fuss about any of it. It was going to be a long, drunken spree recalling the good times, which were many.

I am going to take a little authorial liberty and let you know that I would think back to this afternoon many times in the months and years ahead. It would always feel like the last of something. I counted at least a dozen of the mourners, cherished literary friends, who would be dead within the year, including lovely, sweet Bernie. He was already being claimed by the pancreatic cancer, not that he told any of us, and with him would also go the saloon, dust to dust, how unfair the world is.

Not that I knew any of that at this moment. Jack and I walked into a blur of noise and wet faces and kissed cheeks and slurry condolences. Bernie had three bartenders holding down the fort, yet still they looked up against it, outmanned by our tribe of alcoholic professionals.

Martini in hand, I spotted across the crowded room literary agent Sterling Lord, looking dapper and leonine as ever, even if he was in his early nineties now.

I said to Jack, "Let me introduce you to Sterling. He was Kerouac's agent. He's the man who spent four years searching for a publisher for *On the Road*. He represented Jack to the end and still represents the estate."

I knew Jack would be excited to talk to Sterling, who was an old family friend of course and who in the day had a regular tennis appointment with my father, but I had an ulterior motive.

Carlo Bassi was standing by the jukebox, surveying the scene, alone except for one of his ever-present bodyguards.

"I was wondering when you were going to stroll over here," Carlo said, giving me a nice hug. "Marty was such a classy, old-school gentleman. He was always giving me advice. People forget even when you get to my age we need mentors, people who've been there before us and who can help guide the way."

"Marty, was quite a believer in your gifts, Carlo. It doesn't happen often, but every once in a while someone starts writing late in life—in your case, in your fifties—and it's as if they were born to it. Of course you were a lifelong reader. And your actual life has been filled with more drama than most fiction writers can even begin to make up."

"You look like you want to ask me something," Carlo said.

"Go ahead, I won't bite."

I wanted to ask him to put a hit on Stuart's life, I didn't know what I was waiting for, after all I was standing before the mafia boss nicknamed the Butcher of Astoria. Once even Carlo had visited me at my office to personally hand me an outline for what he called a can't-miss book proposal. The color began to drain from my face as I saw the title, *Body Disposal: A User's Manual.* The queasiness increased as I skimmed chapter headings on the index page, unforgettables like, "The Proper Use of a Woodchipper," and "Sulfuric Acid, a Kitchen Essential," before Carlo let me in on the gag, that he was just messing with me, as he enjoyed saying.

I could not find the words, though, to say the one thing I really wanted to the one man who could really do anything about it. I just wasn't made that way. In the end I said something trite to Carlo like, "I just wanted to hear how the new novel is shaping up…"

"While we have a chance I wanted to tell you something," Carlo said. "I'm glad you're leaving your husband. I know you're not supposed to say this when people break up in case they get together again, but Stuart always struck me as quite insincere. I don't like insincerity, not in books and definitely not in people, either. Because when somebody is being insincere it shows that they don't respect me enough to be able to think I might know the difference."

I realized I had another chance at it. "Actually, Carlo, there is something you can do for me—"

Before I could say another word, Dr. Joyce Rock joined us. Her arm possessed the waist of a lithe, young redhead. "Scotty, Carlo, I wanted to introduce you to my new significant, Paloma DeBlanco. I think she's especially interested in meeting you, Carlo."

"Your novel was so incredible," Paloma gushed. "Oh my God, I couldn't sleep for two days as I had to get to the end of it. And then I couldn't sleep for a week after I finished it because I was still thinking about it. The character of Lanny invaded my dreams— how did you ever come up with her?"

I knew my opportunity was lost, and I mouthed to Carlo we'd pick it up later, not to worry, and I made my way to the bar again, where I collided with Susan Ogden. She was turning one way, I was turning the other.

"I'm so sorry, I know how much Marty meant to you," Susan had the good decency to say.

"Susan, we should talk," I said, deciding, after blowing it with Carlo, not to be a chickenshit again.

"Should we go outside for a moment?" she asked. "I've been dying for a cigarette, anyway."

"You're smoking again?"

"I'm doing everything again," she said with a note of defiance.

Bernie was still standing sentry outside. "My fine ladies, it's against the law to bring your drinks out of the bar."

I said, "We'll just say they're from the Irish pub down the street if asked."

"That works," Bernie said, as we stepped away from him.

Susan shook out a couple of cigarettes from her Newport pack. The drink she carried out was a whiskey sour, her regular. And her favorite authors were Somerset Maugham, Christopher Isherwood, Nabokov, and Alice Munro. In our world that was pretty much all you really needed to know about someone.

The man Susan had been barely registered anymore for me. Sometimes I'd glimpse a memory of Mallon in Susan's broad shoulders. Mallon had been an unprepossessing man with thinning hair and the sad-eyed face of a social services clerk. After Susan underwent the tracheal shave and facial-feminization surgery it was difficult not to study her at times, with the kind of fascination directed towards anyone, really, who has undergone noticeable plastic surgeries—but then that stopped too, and it all just was. Until now. I searched out her face as if I could find her genderless soul, the last thing that leaves us.

"Susan, I know Kent and Stuart are involved with each other."

"I don't think we should have this conversation," she said calmly.

"We were friends, Susan. I always treated you with respect."

"You did."

"Were you and Stuart lovers?"

"Scotty, you did the right thing in getting the restraining order. I can tell you he's enraged and is bellowing to anyone who will listen about how he is going to make your life a living hell for all eternity."

"He was at the chapel today," I said.

Susan only delivered silence.

I said, "I just want to know, were the two of you together all of this time?"

"Scotty, that's part of the disease, the wanting to know. You'll never get to the bottom of it. I'm not going to be your bartender and pour a neat whiskey in a short, squat glass of Hemingway for you. Make it all easy and make it all make sense and make it all go away. And, forgive me for saying this, Scotty, but you are such a self-involved, pampered, over-privileged narcissist that I don't just care to do you any favors."

"Well then," I said, feeling my insides cave in all at once and turning on my heel.

"At least you didn't cut your penis off for him," she said.

Chapter 13

I liked being in the big room as Dalton continued like a locomotive—clickety-clack, clickety-clack, ding—punching out his memoirs. Dalton wrote to jazz music, to Mingus and Coltrane and Miles, and his writing took on that free-flowing misdirection, hitting long notes with the fearless ability to digress elsewhere, unafraid of losing his reader in these tangential outbursts.

Dalton figured, and rightfully so, that if he was interested and entertained by his material than so too would others be.

We all made our home in the living room.

Jack pored over scripts for *Off the Road*. He needed to head back to California in a few days to resume his shooting schedule. He invited me to accompany him, and I've told him I need to think about it.

Without proper explanation, Georgie Guns appeared to be sleeping with Dalton and living in my apartment. Her chosen spot is the Wegner easy chair near the fireplace, where she has been intently tapping out the latest Nicoal Angel thriller on her MacBook Air.

Georgie's sudden appearance seemed to throw off Sadie, who has taken to her room. It made me wonder if Sadie and Dalton had periodic dalliances over the years, which would make sense enough. Sadie had been with me since I was three and when she was twenty-three, you do the math, and even with the natural ravages of time, she remained intact, like the twentieth book in a long-running franchise that refused to falter. My father used to joke with her that she kept a painting of herself in a closet.

When I wasn't delighting in Dalton's new pages, I was final-checking through the galleys for a nonfiction book about the disastrous state of race relations in the country. Called *Surrender No More*, and written by a theologian, it retreated on traditional notions of conflict resolution and seemed weirdly intent on advocating violence in the streets. Oddly, the other book I was editing concurrently was a manuscript by an environmental activist on the front lines of climate change—and it was also a veritable ransom note, this time to the fossil fuel industry, change your evil ways or else.

Now it will never be news that the world can be an ugly, violent, and totally messed-up place. I knew my book-lined study was a fort built with the weakest of fortifications against such ignorance. I would be happy to die as my father and Marty had, knowing that we were on a fool's errand.

Although to me the real insanity were those who spoke, as they did the other day after Marty's service, of making every day count, to live each day as if it would be your last. What a nightmare that would be, everyone telling their own special truth, abandoning their responsibilities, rushing headlong into the abyss. Why, that is what novels were for, conjuring up our worst expectations, careening lives off the rails so that we wouldn't have to—and that is precisely why we owed something to the novelists themselves, who did the same, living without heed to the obvious consequences, even though it all ends crashed into a tree.

I was quite glad when our first round of mimosas arrived, courtesy of Jack. We had waited all the way until one o'clock for our drinks. All of us were bearing down with the work, and the mimosas felt well-earned for a change. At the hour of three we would be released from our tasks because Jack had promised to take us on a special expedition.

The second round of mimosas came promptly at one-twenty. In our favor it should be said that mimosas are a quick and effortless drink and that they have the benefit of orange juice, providing us important vitamin C. The fourth and penultimate round happened just before two-thirty in the afternoon. But before that could happen Jack brought out some hand-rolled joints.

I wanted it to be fun with my new make-believe family, I wanted it to be like when my father was alive, where there were always guests and gaiety, wine and words, but I was not my father, I was something else altogether. I knew I needed to get control of my own personal narrative, I had never veered so off course before. It was all made worse by Stuart. Dalton thought, though he couldn't be positive, that he'd seen Stuart on the sidewalk across the street, stalking. I found myself, drink in hand, jittery and jangled, frequently going to the big windows, checking for myself.

Stuart had initiated multiple new lawsuits against me. He claimed malicious prosecution, that I had issued a false restraining order with no basis in reality. He also accused me of defamation of character and inflicting emotional distress, all a continued outlandishness that I could almost not bear to be exposed to anymore. It would never end. I had made a naive, foolish mistake once, falling in love and trusting another so deeply, and for that there is an awful price.

Somewhere in the haze of the pot and mimosas Georgie said she had some new information for me. I had asked her to give me a possible explanation for the typewriters lodged in Stuart's study.

"I've been doing some research," Georgie said. "And I think I'm on to something."

"How do you find the time, Georgie?" I said, taking a toke. "Sleeping with Dalton, writing your next bestseller, working on real-life detection?"

"I heard you were a crazy bitch when you smoked," she said. "Good to see it with my own eyes."

"Yes, well, there is that," I said in my poor defense.

"Scotty, I think Stuart is making some kind of forgeries. I've seen this thing before. Usually it's a forged legal contract of some sort, like a will that has been altered. The forgers need to make sure that the typewriter and the age of the paper match up with whatever shenanigans that they are up to. The reams of paper in Stuart's cabinets are highly suspect, from all sorts of different mills, most of them out of business from what I can already gather from just doing some minimum internet research—my next step is to do a chemical analysis."

"You know what I think he's doing," Dalton said, his typing come to a halt, "is I think he's forging books."

"That's interesting," Georgie said. "Yes, what about those suddenly-found Leo Gross manuscripts?"

"That's bananas," I said. "Those books are clearly in Gross's own style. How can you fake that writerly DNA?"

"Art forgers do it all the time," Jack said.

"There are a million talented writers out there," Georgie said. "Any one of them could've pulled it off. Think of all the amazing ghostwriters out there who go nameless. Those found novels are bringing in tens of millions of dollars."

"I knew Leo Gross," Dalton said with authority. "Leo Gross would never hold on to a finished novel and shove it in his attic— let alone three of the fucking things. Leo spent it as fast as it came in. He had as many ex-wives as I did. He was just like the rest of us— he wanted money and glory and to buy rounds. He was no saintly J.D. Salinger sitting in some bunker writing for Buddhist posterity."

Georgie was already tapping into some search engine. "Get this, Leo Gross wrote on a Hermes Rocket, circa 1964—which matches up exactly with one of the machines in Stuart's study. I'm going to bet you the other machines match up with other dead authors in Stuart's stable, too. I think big, bad Dalton is all over this."

"I would've made a great private detective, Baby Cakes," he said. "I drink like one at least. And I don't give a shit what people think of me. And like in all those James M. Cain novels trouble knows how to find me."

Chapter 14

Our destination was Northport, Long Island, where Jack Kerouac had lived off and on from 1958-1964. And where every year at Walt's Lounge, one of Kerouac's favored watering holes, they celebrated something called "Jack Kerouac Daze."

We were in the Range Rover on the Long Island Expressway, which was slick with rain and traffic and red taillights, listening to Kerouac speak to us from beyond the grave. I'll explain in a moment. I was in the back seat with Jack, and Dalton was up front with the driver, Hawk, while Georgie decided to stay back at the apartment to work on her novel and to further her investigation. Hawk, who was some kind of kickboxing champion and who doubled as Jack's bodyguard, never said a word. He was a hard, chiseled muscle with a long, blond ponytail, and he was of a type that encouraged fantasies because the reality would pose such an inherent incongruity.

Jack Kerouac was alive in the CD player, his voice traveling to us from the early sixties, from his home in Northport, at the height of his fame. He doesn't seem to be aware that he is being recorded. He's slurry with beer, and at one point he calls out for his mother to make him and his friend a sandwich. A kind of sweetness and naive curiosity constitute his very fabric. He is also quite brilliant, as he dances merrily on any subject, Celine, world history, Russian novelists, St. Augustine, he can go from speaking French to Latin to English, all the while making deep philosophic points about the Catholic Church, Eastern religions, and the Yankees-Red Sox rivalry.

We clicked him off, as we left the expressway behind and closed in on Northport. Jack said, "Crazy isn't it that the author of *On the Road* is living with his mom and he doesn't even drive a car."

"Poor bastard," Dalton said. "I visited him here a couple of times. His mom would give him an allowance—a roll of nickels to go out with at night."

We drove down Main Street towards the harbor. Northport was the kind of quaint, sweet-feeling town that you immediately thought, I could live here, this would be nice, I could make it work here. The little shops, the steepled churches, the old-fashioned columned bank, the diners and restaurants lit with little white Christmasy lights, the forgotten trolly tracks, the smell of the sea, the sense of continuing generations.

"Whaling town from the 1600s," Dalton said. "Back when Kerouac lived here it wasn't so upscale. Half the shops on Main Street were boarded up because of the hard times. Kerouac liked it that way, reminded him of Lowell. But closer to New York City."

Hawk pulled the Range Rover into the lot near the town docks. There was a picturesque park with a band stand, the trees golden and wistful, all of it looking out at the lobster boats swaying on the silvery waters of the Sound. We got out, the rain had just stopped and it was a purple, raw-bruised dusk, the clouds were scurrying away, and everything smelled freshly hopeful, the pavement slick with newly fallen leaves. Jack led us to one of the waterview restaurants, it didn't seem to matter which one you picked, they all looked like fine choices.

Our hostess gasped when we walked in. "Oh, my fucking God," she exclaimed, staring at Jack. "Excuse my language. It's you, Jack Kerouac."

"Hey, he's not the only one who's famous around here," Dalton felt obliged to say. "But what I'd do to look like this fellow here," he said, clasping Jack's shoulder.

We were led to a table that looked out at a flotilla of docked sailboats. Hawk took a seat at the bar, from which to watch over us. Another pretty college co-ed came with our menus. "What can I start you off with?" she said, her eyes only for Jack.

Dalton said, "Bring us a round of Old Fashioneds." When she left, Dalton said, "Important to vary your drink selection. Otherwise you can turn into an alcoholic. We're voluptuaries, which is very different. Sampling the many good things in life, not beholden to any one thing."

After our drinks arrived, our waitress began to recite the specials. "We have fresh bluefish today and—"

"We'll certainly try some of that," Dalton said, cutting her off.

"Our chef also as a soft-shell-crab starter—"

"Lovely," Dalton said, already finishing his first drink. "Three orders of that for sure."

"And there's a special fra diavolo with linguini and lobster and—"

"Sold," Dalton said.

"And we also have a chateaubriand for two—"

"How can we resist?" Dalton said. "We'll need another round of these fine cocktails, too. Along with the wine list."

The college waitress was starting to look a little confused. "I think you may have ordered too many main dishes."

"Nonsense," Dalton said. "What we don't eat, we'll take home, we're not wasters."

Studying the menu with the practiced eye of a James Beard, Dalton thickened the confusion by insisting on the additions of rigatoni veal bolognese and oysters Rockefeller. He then pushed further, "But of course we'll start with the endive salad with gorgonzola and the grilled portobellos with goat cheese."

The exasperated waitress said, "We'll never fit it all on the table."

"Why, get us another table then," Dalton commanded. "It's

not every night you have Jack Kerouac and his entourage in the restaurant. But first bring us some of the bruschetta and a couple of bottles of your finest Barolo."

After she left, Dalton turned to me and said, "Do you remember the worst book I ever wrote?"

I waited, I didn't dare say a thing. He said, *"Dalton Ford's Favorite Dishes from the French Mediterranean.* What a lark, what a crock. I begged your dear father for that assignment. The funny thing is, I didn't even write it."

"Really? I had no idea. It seemed in your style."

"Kit, my son from marriage number three, wrote it. I gave him half the advance money and we bonded in Nice and Cannes over extravagant dinners your father essentially paid for. Kit was a good writer, but the publishers kept turning him down, killing his soul."

"What's Kit doing now?"

"He's the chief restaurant critic for *The Los Angeles Times,*" Dalton said, guffawing.

Jack said, "Scotty, think what we were talking about earlier, see how easy it is to fake a book. Nobody guessed that Dalton didn't write it."

It strangely unnerved me to think about the faking of books. Now in essence the entire structure of a novel is an elaborate ruse and artifice, but it is those intimate, vulnerable, connecting voices in our novels that allow us to go behind the veneer to find the human in us. Of course my sociopathic husband would pervert such a beautiful thing. After all, Stuart himself was a fake. He assumed everyone was as reptilian as he was, that the only true voice was just get what you want any which way you can do it and just assume the worst about others, too, that they were just like you.

I shuddered to think of Stuart, and even as removed as we were, out on the Island, I found myself looking up every time a new customer came through the door, eternally on guard, as if at any moment there would be strangulating hands around my neck. Even the appearance of the wine didn't help, not that I didn't drink it with a certain purpose. I wanted it all to be bright and fun and warmly incoherent. But I couldn't seem to make it so. Jack became quite irritated with me. He tried to give me those funny pills again to stay awake.

"I don't want to," I told him. "I don't feel safe right now. Can't you understand that?"

"They're not really bennies. They're just caffeine and ginkgo biloba."

"I just need to feel safe," I said again.

"You're just not paying attention," Jack said. "And I want to say something, and I don't want you to take it the wrong way, but I don't think you respect me enough."

I gulped more wine and waited in anticipation of this new turn. "I'm a serious person," he said so sadly. "Scotty, you haven't even taken a moment to open up my novel. You read everybody else's books. Why won't you take the time for me?"

I said, "It's a very serious thing to read the novel of someone close to you. What if I don't like it? Have you thought of that?"

I flashed on my first real boyfriend, Clem, who I met sophomore year at college. I was enamored with his cashmere v-neck sweaters, his fondness for the juniper berry, and other F. Scott-imitative ways. Clem had written a novel on summer break called *Rock Lyric*, the whole thing told in the repetitive stanzas of a pop song, and before I read it I was hopelessly in love with him. After reading his drivel, though, I knew there was no hope for the relationship and I ended it with alacrity.

Jack said, "We've had sex. We've already been intimate. All I'm doing is asking you to read my novel."

"Sex is not intimate," Dalton proclaimed. "Anyone can have sex, and all sorts of talentless people do so all the time. There is no genius in spreading legs and insertion. Writing a novel on the other hand requires exquisite care and craftsmanship."

"I concur," I said. "A novel is all about the withholding of reward and instant gratification. It is the opposite of sex."

Jack became sullen, and soon took to openly flirting with the hostess and waitress, who both continued to keep checking in on his comfort. Harmony and Ashley, they had names.

Men were always behaving badly, at least it felt rare for it to be any other way. It was finally, always, all about them, their egos, their feelings, their penises, why, it was a gender of narcissism. No wonder there were so many male writers, since writing itself was an act of unfiltered self-absorption, to believe that your words, your life, matter more than the trials of others.

We left the restaurant, Dalton and Jack in front, and Hawk and I trailing behind. Hawk carried two shopping bags of leftovers.

"He's a jerk," Hawk said, his first words to me. "Actors, they all get this way. It's not your fault."

"Who's your favorite writer?" I inquired.

"Richard Ford," Hawk said, surprising me with his rather excellent choice. "*Rock Springs* is a small masterpiece."

Walt's Lounge, which was right on Main Street, was a mad house, crowded with Kerouac addicts and locals—lobstermen and clammers and the curious—as well as a gaggle of septuagenarians, who I supposed were there to provide the memory heroin.

Jack was greeted by rowdy cheers, and he was crowd surfed to the back of the bar. That was the last I would see of Jack and Hawk for a while. Fortunately, Dalton was there to take care of me. We sat out of the way by the storefront windows, drinking Rusty Nails, which Dalton described as a fetching mix of Scotch whisky and Drambuie and lemon juice. "It fights off the scurvy," he added.

A makeshift stage and microphone had been set up in the back of the lounge. And people took turns either reading from Kerouac's novel *Big Sur* or sharing personal recollections of the man.

Kerouac's lonely and disheveled spirit haunted Walt's Lounge. His face stared at us from a dozen or so photographs that fought for space among the sports pennants and beer mirrors. Odd to see Kerouac and Burroughs and Ginsberg at a Memorial Day parade, looking outrageously out of time and place among the suburban conformists, waving their little American flags. And then there was Kerouac himself, or at least a life-size wax figure of him, spookily leaning against the bar, hoisting one last beer to eternity.

Walt's was its own wax museum, with its red vinyl stools, its ancient jukebox and cigarette machine still aglow, the ruined felt of the blue pool table, the pissy, yeasty smell of the taps, vestiges of all that two-in-the-morning loneliness, an endless march of nights that finally ends for everybody.

Kerouac, I soon learned, walked around town like a ghost of a man at all hours of night barefoot or in his battered bedroom slippers. His phantasmic nocturnes were the stuff of local legend, and most of the cobwebby stories revolved around drinking and foolish before-dawn hijinks. One of the old codgers at the mic was telling about the time he and Kerouac went skinny-dipping off the town dock at two in the morning one November night because why the hell not.

Rumson, the white-haired owner, gnarly as an old oak, stopped by our table. He seemed to actually remember Dalton. "Nice seeing you in here again, sir."

"Love the changes you've made to the place," Dalton said deadpan.

Rumson pointed to the stage. "That's Freddy Bayou up there, used to be a serious sculptor. Same stupid stories every year. The man makes a living on the college lecture circuit recalling his marvelous friendship with Kerouac. Why, Freddy hardly knew Kerouac. First he tells that dumb old skinny-dipping story, then the next one is going to be the time he and Jack borrowed a fire engine because why the hell not. Although I shouldn't be one to talk, half my business these days seems to come from Kerouac seekers who get some special pleasure pounding back a brewski in Jack's old haunt."

"Who knew Kerouac was destined for the museums," Dalton said.

"What a royal pain in the ass he was when he was making the rounds, coming here and in Gunther's and Murphy's. I'm only sorry I didn't hold on to the signed first editions he gave me for payment when he was decidedly low on cash."

"Shame," Dalton said. "Probably worth many thousands today."

"You never can tell," Rumson said. "I named this lounge for the poet Walt Whitman, who was born just a few miles away. Kerouac was his own version of it. Traveling across the country with that scroll in his knapsack. Lot like Whitman, taking odd jobs, a blue-collar voice of the people, his buddhism like Walt's transcendentalism, the sexual confusion, the body electric and all that. They both kept writing the same book over and over again, if anyone bothered to ask me."

Dalton said, "Kerouac was influenced by everybody— James Joyce, Thomas Wolfe, the Bible, Henry Miller, Celine, Fitzgerald— but somehow every word is just him, unmistakably distilled by Jack. I think that's partially why he lives on. In our corporate age of obedience he gave reign to his own immortal soul."

"Fancy words for a self-described drunk," Rumson said.

Mike McGrady, the newspaperman who had been behind the *Naked Came the Stranger* hoax, was introduced to the stage.

"I didn't even know Mike was still alive," I said.

Dalton said, "Mike came out to Montana, must be forty years ago, to do a magazine piece on me. Quite a great guy, we had a rousing time. Good to see him looking so vigorous."

Mike, a Northportite, told a funny little story about how he first got to know Kerouac through his plumber. The plumber kept telling him that there was another writer fella by the name of Carrot living in Northport and would he like to be introduced to him.

"Well, as you might imagine," Mike said, "I had no idea who this Mr. Jack Carrot might be. But I was young and just starting out and said sure I'd like to meet him. I can tell you my wife Corinne and I were slightly surprised to walk into this Mr. Carrot's house and find out the plumber had screwed up his name. Jack Kerouac only happened to be about the most famous writer in the country in 1959."

Writing, Mike explained, wasn't just about reading others and doing the hard work of sitting down to the typewriter, it was also about actually meeting other writers, getting the chance to talk to them and to benefit from their struggles, to even know that this kind of life was actually possible, to make the dream smaller so that it could be approachable.

A little later Mike and his wife Corinne joined us. And Dalton was off and running, "Good Jesus, man, how many years has it been, Mike? What a bender we went on in Whitefish, I can't believe we're still here to tell about it. What are you drinking, Mike? Jack Daniel's, isn't it? Jacks all around."

The boozy evening got boozier, a retreat into long-ago whiskey nights, as Mike and Dalton transported back to New Haven in the nineteen-fifties. Mike had studied under the poet and novelist Robert Penn Warren. Dalton had also gone to Yale, a few years after Mike, and he had taken writing classes with John Hersey, the author of *Hiroshima*.

"The man invented the New Journalism," Dalton said. "Who even knows who he is today?"

Corinne, who had to be in her seventies, looked practically ageless with a beauty that seemed preserved in the amber of self-knowledge. "These Kerouac remembrances," she told me behind the voices of the men, "always make me so sad. Jack was such a sweet, sweet man but so lost. I have photos with Jack bouncing my baby son Sean on his lap—and I can hardly bear to look at them now. Jack was so gentle with him. That sweetness…"

Her voice trailed off and I saw that tears were gathering. "You have no idea," she began again. "Once he was over our house after he'd been jailed for vagrancy on Fire Island. He hadn't eaten in several days and I made him this terrible, burned omelet, I hadn't yet become the gourmet, and he kept telling me it was the best thing he had ever eaten. That poor, sweet soul—he was just not there on some level for himself. I miss him, you have to remember he was a real person to us. These were real people."

Then Corinne reached for my hand and took it for the briefest moment. She said, "Are you doing okay? You look a little lost yourself."

Thankfully I could see my Jack trying to navigate his way to us, through the crush of bodies, continually besieged by drunken admirers. Many of them were carrying paperback copies of Jack Kerouac's novels, and I witnessed the strangeness of a TV actor being asked to sign them as if he were the real author.

When Jack made it to our table, he said, "Let's roll. We're going to Kerouac's house—surprise, surprise—the real one where he used to live. It's all arranged. We're going to have a party there."

Mike said, "Kerouac himself wrote, 'The best of things must be that they end.' That's from his novel *Tristessa*."

"Tell you the truth, Mike," Dalton said, "I never really cottoned to his books."

And then we were rolling, a big, crazy group of us spilling outside onto the sidewalk like beer freed from a bottle, with Jack shouting out directions. People were getting into cars all around us, and they were honking horns and yelling unintelligible war cries as they blasted away. Moments later Hawk was pulling alongside us in the Range Rover. Somehow we had lost Dalton and the McGradys.

"Don't you worry," Jack told me, "Mike's got his own chauffeured car."

"Dalton was so excited to see Mike tonight. They knew each other in the old days."

Jack started laughing. "Oh, shit. That's so fucked up. I should've told you. The real Mike McGrady died a few years back. The guy you were talking to is an actor on our show—he narrates from the present day. That old dude keeps it in character always. Then there's a young Mike McGrady who plays alongside me back in the nineteen-sixties."

"What about Corinne? Was she real?"

"Far as I know," said Jack.

I was suddenly overcome with sadness and nausea. I said almost in the way of pleading, "Please don't tell Dalton. It would break his heart."

My stomach was swimming, and I stopped myself from getting into the Rover. "What's wrong, Scotty?" Jack said. What's wrong was that I was retching. I moved away from Walt's Lounge, took a few steps into an alley, away from the street lamps and the glare of headlights, and then it was all that awfulness. It was a purging of drink and food and all that lonely, fetid nostalgia. I was a wobbly mess, my face wet with the exertions and tears, my soul in transit. Jack came to me and comforted me with what men always say in a spot, which is don't worry, baby, it's going to be okay. At that moment I didn't think anything was going to be okay again, I just felt the cold fall night gripping me, and imagined perversely that I was probably just one of thousands over the years who had vomited here on this exact same piece of pavement and then needed help getting into a car.

Chapter 15

Kerouac's old house was only a couple of minutes away, close enough for him to float down to Main Street on his nightly hauntings. I was already beginning to feel better with the fresh air gushing through the open windows of the Rover. We entered a street of pleasant colonials and splanches set back on manicured lawns, the picture of conventional mores, hard to imagine Kerouac living here and not the bohemian excesses of New York, the way he once did and which is more easily summoned.

Kerouac's split-level, funnily with two garages, was already a bright scene of anarchy, at least a dozen strangers waiting by the door with cases of beer, smoking cigarettes and joints, the lawn and street choked with cars. There was a flood-lit backboard in the driveway, and Dalton and the actor who plays Mike McGrady had found a basketball and were taking one-handed errant shots—each of them cupping a Budweiser in their free hand—their misses bouncing off parked vehicles.

"High school kids used to come down here looking for him," my Jack said. "They'd throw pebbles at his window to try to get him to come out and play with them. And Kerouac hated it because the kids were always disappointed when they met him and saw that he no longer looked like the young handsome stud of his book jackets."

"Maybe that will happen to you someday," I said, more cruelly than intended.

Jack took me by the hand and we stumbled to the front door to wild cheers in the moonlit suburban night. I noted the waitresses from the restaurant earlier—Harmony and Ashley—were part of Jack's oddly collected retinue, which included dudes with their guitars and rough-hewn baymen and blue girls who were streaming too much makeup and didn't quite look old enough to drink. Someone handed me a beer, and I unsnapped it and slugged some back.

Jack searched for the house key under the welcome mat. "Damn," he said, "this is where they told me it would be." Then he checked under some of the planters on the porch and finally reeled it in from beneath a large pumpkin left out in anticipation of Halloween. More cheers. And then we stampeded into the house and made ourselves a little too comfortable. The liquor cabinet was broken into. There was the sizzle and smell of eggs and bacon being cooked up in the kitchen. The musicians plopped down on the expensive sofas and began to play early Bob Dylan songs. The Queen Anne living room gathered the smoky haze of an opium den in mere minutes.

I lost all sense of time, of course. Someone handed me a Campari on ice, and it became my drink of choice for the rest of the night. Dalton and Mike engineered a poker game in the dining room. The baymen looked to be losing their life's savings in there, to deduce by the piles of cash in front of Dalton and Mike. The two of them played a wacky, determined game of no-limit, five-card draw, raising without heed, never even bothering to glance at their cards. Dalton and Mike took turns letting the other win. The baymen kept folding their cards, every single time, not smart enough to actually call either of them on their bluffs.

Finally one of the knotty, sinewy men had had enough. He put another hundred into the pot and said, "I got to see for myself what you have there, amigo. I'm calling you this time for sure."

Dalton turned his cards over one by one, as blindly unknowing as his opponent was. He flipped over four natural kings.

The bayman said, "Crap, you guys always have it."

"Of course I have it," Dalton said, smiling widely. "I play a most conservative game, in poker and in life."

I drifted back into the living room and I was aware that Jack was missing from the scene, just as Harmony and Ashley were nowhere to be found. I just knew, and I didn't know why I knew, but I knew in the way of a novelist who has drawn a character and plotted out a certain trajectory, only to have the character defy that original outline. I had always known who Jack was, his true, deep character, and when I climbed the stairs and heard the rude noises coming from one of the open bedrooms, I was not shocked because it was in keeping with what I already knew about him.

I veered into another bedroom, I was tired, I was not even really vexed with Jack, and I may even have been relieved, better to find out now than in a later when such a thing would rip me open. I wanted to crash and to wake in another, far different day. Before I could fall asleep, though, the door opened to reveal Jack. He shirt was half unbuttoned, and I wasn't sure what to think. He fell in next to me though on the bed. I don't really remember much about what happened next. I think I asked him if he had been in the other bedroom with those girls. And I think he told me that Hawk was in there. That's what I think happened.

Chapter 16

In the late late morning, or maybe it was already afternoon, I became aware of Jack lying next to me and snoring deeply. That was just before we were roused by the cops.

A Northport police officer stood at the door to the bedroom and said, "Do you folks happen to know where you are?"

Jack was coming to and he said, "This is Jack Kerouac's old house."

"It's one of them," he said.

"I don't understand the problem. We absolutely have permission to be here."

"Not according to the owners," the officer said. "I'm going to need both of you to get dressed now."

Downstairs there were four other police officers taking statements from the party survivors. I didn't see Hawk or Dalton about. One officer busied himself with a dv camera filming the wreckage, the overturned tables, the broken glasses, the wine-splashed ivory carpeting, the smashed-in flat screen, the cigarette butts floating in the fish tank—and that was just the living room. Someone had also taken the time to scrawl on one of the walls in black marker the first page, sentence by sentence, of *On the Road*, in apparent tribute.

Now we did get to the bottom of the confusion, sort of and eventually. It took some time to convince the police and the owners, who were in vacant-eyed disbelief at the wreckage of their home, having just returned from an overnight wedding in Pennsylvania, that it was all an innocent, if outrageous, misunderstanding.

What Jack didn't seem to know was that Kerouac in his short time in Northport had lived in three different houses. The first house had been on Gilbert Street, the next one on Earl, and the final one on Judy Ann Court. Kerouac kept changing addresses because the fame vultures would eventually find him and circle, pecking away at his privacy, until he was forced to pick up and move once again.

Jack told the cops that he knew Karen and Bobby, who indeed seemed to be the owners of one of the Kerouac houses, just not this one.

"Last night at the bar I just asked some people where Kerouac lived and this is how we got here," Jack said. "Had no idea, man, that this wasn't Karen and Bobby's place. Super sorry."

We weren't going to get off that easy. The house was trashed, yes, there was that garden variety offense. Then there were the college kids, or maybe they were high school age, who knew, but they were clearly one way or the other under the legal drinking age, sleeping it off on the couches that now reeked of cannabis. The owners' two beloved house cats, Josie and Fritz, who had never once ventured outside in their lives, were unaccounted for. Of course there was also the matter of their basketball-dented Audi sedan out front. Also, worst of all for us, the current owners weren't Jack Kerouac fans, not of the show, not of the books.

Jack and I were the only ones arrested, I suspect because we were the only ones who looked like we could pay for the damage. An officer put us in handcuffs and led us out to one of the multiple cruisers silently flashing blue in the drive.

"Did you know the writer Eugene O'Neill also lived at one time in Northport," the cop said, turning the ignition. "Too bad you're not an O'Neill fan. He only had the one house down on Asharoken."

"I was Jamie in *Long Day's Journey into Night*," Jack said sadly. "We did it at the Long Wharf Theater."

"Morphine addiction, alcoholism," I said. "We're almost there."

We were brought down to the village police station, where we were politely fingerprinted and photographed and booked. We were charged with illegal trespassing, breaking and entering, vandalism, possession of a controlled substance, and contributing to the delinquency of minors.

It would take some hours before Leyton Smulders could arrange to bail us out. For that duration Jack and I were put in separate holding cells, which in consideration of the night's events struck me as ideal.

Not that I knew it yet, but at the same time Lizza Morris was being put in her own holding tank at Bellevue Hospital, awaiting psychiatric evaluation.

Lizza, her coat pockets loaded down with heavy stones, like her hero Virginia Woolf, had leaped into her own river, the East River, to drown the sorrows of her broken marriage. She was saved by a good samaritan who jumped in after her.

I would find myself in the days to come envious of Lizza, that she could love so fiercely, feel so deeply, leaving me to wonder about my own lack of initiative around Jack.

Chapter 17

Jack's novel wasn't terrible. It was made less terrible by the little bottles of Bombay Sapphire that we kept emptying into our plastic cups of tonic water, although frankly I was slightly ashamed that I had already broken my promise to myself to drink less after the disaster of Northport.

I was almost done with the book, I was scanning through it on my iPad, and I knew Jack was crazy keen to hear my opinion. Because of our close proximity—we were in adjoining seats on a Virgin flight to Los Angeles, of course first class, which was no different than coach to Jack, we had almost taken a private jet— he was able to keep sneaking looks over to see what page I had progressed to.

It was an autobiographical novel, and there was a surreal quality to it because Jack had not bothered to change the names. For example I was a little shocked to learn that his twin sister is actually named Elsie, yes, after my mother. Even Bumby and I are in the book in a peripheral way, as a kind of bizarre totem, representing a parallel universe of psychic destruction, all ignited by Jack's father.

At its best the novel had the hollowed-out, rich-kid-ennui feeling of *Less Than Zero*. At its worst there was an amateurishness that would take years to evolve through, and I personally did not know whether I had it in me to take that long journey with Jack. As I say the novel wasn't terrible, and it certainly was publishable because of Jack's name recognition. I mean, we would never have accepted it if it was a book by an unknown, but Jack was Jack, and that was enough.

I put the iPad away, and he was all bright-eyed silly expectation. I did not have the heart to hurt him, so I decided to do what my father often advised in similar situations, which was to just tell a lovely happy lie, far better to do that than to offer a searing critique that did no one any real good. If I had told Jack the honest truth, it would've destroyed him, after all he did not have the talent yet to make the necessary edits to the novel, or even the capacity for such self analysis.

Why was it anyway that people wanted honest opinions of their work? They did not demand it in other parts of their gamey, elusive lives. Look at us, for example. Jack and I had not discussed at all what had happened in Kerouac's house. Did Jack do something with those college girls? Had I imagined it? Should we have a forthright sit-down about what it all might mean? Should we discuss our own character arcs and if such tawdriness was really necessary to the development of our story?

Hawk was seated several rows behind us, intently enjoying a used-bookstore copy of Joan Didion's *Play it as it Lays*, and as much as I admired Hawk's literary tastes, it was wonderfully clear he would never be discussing what happened the other night, either. Hawk had brilliantly shown his ability to compartmentalize and to move on from the experience, whatever it was, as if it was just another driving assignment.

"Jack," I finally said, at the beginning of our descent, "your novel absolutely blew me away. An unforgettable reading experience."

"I'm so relieved," he said, actually sounding it. "I put everything I had into it. Everything I know and probably will ever know is in that novel."

"It really shows, Jack. I look forward to publishing it."

"What did you like best about it?" he asked with the innocence of a boy half his age.

"That you wrote it, Jack. That it has your name on it."

Los Angeles looked obscenely beautiful from the air, set on a dusky orange glow of desert, framed by mountains that were like crystals, the dark towers of downtown to the right of us, more of a cityscape than I would've guessed from the novels, then all those swimming pools like tiny backyard inkwells, more gorgeous unexpected mountains, then the gasp of the wild green Pacific, here we come.

Jack kept another Rover here, and even though he was eager to get home, I asked for a favor. We took a side trip to Santa Monica, eight miles up the Pacific Coast Highway, thirty lost minutes in a lifetime of ticks and tocks that don't aways make the most sense.

We drove ultra slowly down Ocean Avenue when we got there. It reminded me of the Promenade de la Croisette in Cannes, which was a place my father had taken me once—for the film festival, one of our titles had made it to the screen—all those high-end shops, the restaurants with their valets, the diffident apartment buildings and hotels with their red-suited doormen standing guard, the giant, regal palms lining either side of the wide thoroughfare, all that sunlit money.

I wanted to see where my mother had died, you can understand that. It was a bleached white edifice with deco emerald windows, a bright flash of light across the street from the wind-blown ocean, but just a building in the end, I'm not sure what I expected. I tried to imagine my mother walking on the beach, but I could not even conjure that threadbare sketch.

I had come west because it was time to put the ghosts of the past to rest, that it was this gift of absolution that Jack really offered me. I also needed a short blue-skied mini-vacation, away from my spigot of legal troubles. The clean-up of the charges from our Northport debacle, what Jack was now calling on his Facebook page a "literary salon gone badly awry," looked to be more absurdly complicated that at first considered. Leyton, ordinarily possessed of Job-like patience, let me know that I need not to invite any new trouble in. He was concerned that our hijinks had already greatly effected the potential sale price of Dorian and Cage. The executor and the estate of Martin Cage, as expected, were looking for a quick liquidation of all assets.

"Do you want to go inside the hotel?" Jack asked, the Rover in pause mode.

I stared up at the bleached exterior with as much intensity as I could muster, as if the act of supremely focusing would reveal the mysteries behind the facade. I wished without any real hope that I could even imagine my mother, let alone know her. I wondered if she was looking down at me from whatever heaven there is, worried for the sake of her little girl.

"Let's roll," I said, hoping to sound brave for once like Jack.

Jack's house was in Beachwood Canyon, in what I learned was the Hollywood Hills, and you had to crawl up all these narrow winding side streets, good luck finding your way without a navigational instrument, weaving to the top of this Eden, amazingly flush and tropical, the pinks and purples and scarlets and yellows of the wild flowers, blooming everywhere on the hillside, an explosion of warm, luscious sexuality, no wonder my mother loved it out here.

Jack took the time to name them for me, verbena and snapdragon he said, evening primrose and morning glory, scarlet larkspur and bougainvillea, as sexy to me as if he was naming nineteenth-century Russian and American writers that I had yet to hear of. I liked that our roles were reversing, here in paradise, Jack was in charge, he knew things I did not, he was master and commander.

I knew so little about the world we were about to enter. California for me was the novellas of Nathaniel West, the Pat Hobby stories, the detective noirs of Mulholland Drive, and, yes, the deadly and arid languor of Joan Didion and Bret Easton Ellis.

From the street it was impossible to comprehend the size of Jack's house, just a tall wooden gate protecting a sheer wall of cracked stucco, teal blue shutters and window boxes, creeping ivy, a sense of being in a village in Provence, that foreign and that time lost.

Inside was a surprise, to say the least. It was a mansion, airy and fragrant with citrus, with multiple levels of sunny perfection, with French doors open to the patio and the glittering swimming pool and the lemon trees, all built into a cliff with panoramic views of the parched canyon and the Hollywood sign and then beyond to the spires of the black city and then beyond that even, all the way to the clouds rolling over the invisible sea.

That the house was fabulous should not be a surprise. What shocked me actually were the Danish furnishings, couches and chairs that were exact replicas of the ones found in our Fifth Avenue apartment. There were even gloomily romantic Hudson River School paintings that only my mother would've picked out, and they served as counter points to the big, bright David Hockneys that I assumed Jack's father had purchased.

"This is your father's house, isn't it?" I said to Jack. "My mother had to have picked out the furniture, it's so her taste. How come she was in a hotel when she died?"

"They were putting the pool in at the time," Jack said, sheepishly. "Renovating. I should've told you. I'm sorry. This is our family compound. My sister lives here, too."

"Is your father home?" I said, almost as if it was an urgent hope that he was.

"Dad's in Maui. He surfs. We keep a place there, too. He may be back in a couple of days, depends on the wave conditions."

"You've never mentioned your mother, Jack. I was curious about that when I was reading your novel. She's not in it. I mean, I know she married your father and had you and Elsie but other than that you've said nothing. Where is she?"

Hawk stood behind us, holding our bags, silently waiting.

"It's not a good story," Jack said. "Let me take you to your room first."

This was the first I had heard that I would not be staying in Jack's room. I followed Jack up the stairs, and Hawk followed us like a bellhop, to a palatial guest suite with a private balcony. I don't know why I knew it, but I did—it was my mother's room. Stepping in there I became conscious of, as if by magic wand, a great easing of my burden. I do not know if you will be accepting of this or not, but I experienced a warm sensation of being truly watched over, a kind of instant serenity. I've read passages in many books where we are asked to believe in an inner change, a moment of character metamorphosis that seems unlikely—and yet here I will ask of you to believe that it was thus for me, not that I can truly explain it or fathom it, it just was.

"This was your mother's private space," Jack said after dismissing Hawk and anticipating me. "She used it as an office. She was writing another novel in here just before she died."

I sat on the edge of the bed, beginning to breathe it all in, and before I knew it, I couldn't stop myself and I began to sob uncontrollably. Jack sat beside me and put his arm around me and did his best to comfort me, but I kept going for a while, I had held so much in for so long and held so much together for so many others for so long that the rain burst of my tears refused to diminish. I was a flash-flood river, washing away everything with me, violent fast eradicating.

I don't know how long it took for the heaving to stop and for me to regain my reasoned self, but when I did I felt different, cool and distant among the river corpses. My inside landscape seemed to shift, revealing new mesas.

"Jack," I said as calmly composed as I have ever been, "how many people have you slept with?"

"You don't want to know that, Scotty."

"Jack, I was sexually abused as a child and I do want to know it."

"I don't understand, what do these things have in common?"

"I have lived and breathed too long underwater. You have no

idea what it is to feel so slow moving and muffled, to exist in a place where so little light filters through and you just become accustomed to the murky depths. If my mother had lived, surely she would've seen and known in a way my father was simply incapable of."

"I can relate to that," Jack said.

"I was destroyed as a child, and I'm just begining to not hate myself."

"I've slept with over a hundred people," he determined, moving with me in this new direction. "I'm not sure exactly how many, maybe a hundred and fifty."

"That wasn't so hard, was it?"

"Hard enough."

"I just don't want to be afraid to ask questions anymore. Now tell me what happened in Kerouac's house with those two girls from the restaurant. Let's let the truth set us free."

"They...we didn't have sex. I watched them with each other. I asked them to do that for me."

"I see," I said, not really seeing but wanting to find a generous place in my heart. "And why don't you want me to stay with you in your bedroom?"

"My father and my sister don't know that we've been intimate. It would cause a certain amount of confusion."

"Jack, when were you going to tell me all of this?"

"I didn't have a plan, you know," he said. "I just don't work that way. Are you mad at me, Scotty?"

The odd thing was, I was the opposite of mad, I felt insanely free, as if I could do anything, ask any question, live any life. I was pleased that we could have this forward conversation. I had put a lot on Jack, and I knew that. He had got me here to California, and if he did nothing else for me ever, I would still be grateful.

"Jack, you are a true, sweet angel walking this earth. What happened to your own mother?"

"She left us," Jack said. "Our mother was an actress. She got involved with someone she met on set."

"How old were you?"

"I was the same age you were when your own mother left you. Isn't that a screwed-up coincidence? I was three years old. I don't remember my mom much. She drowned in someone's swimming pool with no one around to save her, she'd been drinking, there was cocaine in her system."

"I'm so sorry, Jack," I said, reaching for his hand.

He began to choke up. "I couldn't write about it," he said, the tears evolving into rivulets. "I wanted to, I really wanted to go there and find it so I could understand it and really move on from it. But I didn't have the skill to go there as a beginning novelist."

Chapter 18

I will always remember the first time I saw her. I took a nap in my mother's old room, how lovely is that to say, and when I came to, feeling revitalized and remarkably lucid, I saw Jack's sister standing there. Elsie appeared in a halo of granulated sunlight at the foot of my bed. I knew it was Elsie because she looked so much like Jack, black haired with eyes as artificially blue as Windex, compact and unapologetically carefree, born of a confidence that I knew little about but which attracted me like a drunken moth whirling in candlelight. Yes, it was a kind of love at first sight, even if such things should not be believed in.

"I'm Elsie," she said. "I could not wait any longer to see you."

I got up from the bed, I was half naked, just in my undergarments, and yet I moved to her with ease and she received me in her embrace without hesitation. Isn't it interesting how the inevitable feels? You do not question it, it just happens like the way the sun comes out after a heavy rain, it is somehow obvious and ordinary and yet everything feels changed. Actually, I am downplaying this too much, it was even more miraculous than all that. It was the way of snow falling out of a hot blue sky, wild and otherworldly.

I don't remember what we exactly said, I remember her telling me something about people coming over, a party that night, and I said something along the lines of that I didn't have anything to wear. My clothes were all dark and too formal, fine on the East Coast, but not feeling right in this orange-blossom paradise. We were almost the exact size, Elsie and me, and she took me to her room and into her closet and she dressed me and it did not feel at all strange.

Her clothes fit me perfectly, and in minutes I was feeling un-tight and loose-limbed, in light linen and cotton, airily transformed. She placed turquoise around my neck and wrists. She had the absolute right pair of sandals for me. I felt the way it must feel to have a sister or a best girlfriend, something previously unknown to me. I studied myself in the dressing room mirror and in the reflection of her pleased eyes, its own kind of narcissism and reward.

I suppose this is where my story truly begins. There was the beginning of an important new relationship that would last the rest of my days. This was the first real coming to terms with what had been in me always. And, when I would look back years from now, it was the beginning of the self that would endure and gallop the final furlongs of my life.

I have a memory of studying the books and scripts that seemed to be stacked everywhere, swamping Elsie's nightstands and tables and bedroom shelves, how much I wanted to pass positive judgment. Females far outnumbered writerly male chromosomes, the Brontes and Austin, Rebecca West and Elizabeth Bowen, Margaret Atwood and AM Homes, Zadie Smith and Shirley Hazzard, Penelope Fitzgerald and Meg Wolitzer, on and on, great walls of chick lit and feminist theory, how different from my own library.

Of course she also maintained the complete works of Jack Kerouac. Elsie, I would shortly learn, was her brother's manager, as well as the true creator and writer of *Off the Road*. Her Emmy and her Golden Globe were whimsically displayed in a downstairs guest bathroom, on a shelf that also held a junior varsity soccer trophy and winning ribbon from a middle school spelling bee.

We reclined on chaises on the veranda before the guests arrived, watching the sun die on the canyon, the off-key yowls of coyotes like misbegotten music, as we sipped a buttery Napa chardonnay, which was not something we drank much of in the New York autumn but which would later become my favorite, talking quietly as if every sentence imparted a great intimacy.

"Don't worry, Scotty, you're safe with us," she said, and that was truly what I was feeling and thinking. Stuart couldn't reach me here in the California dusk, it was too beautiful for all that, the red shimmer on the pool, the coolness of early evening, the drifting smoke of our cigarettes, that sense of being part of forever.

"Stuart will try to kill me," I told Elsie.

"I wish he were dead," she replied. "And all your troubles were gone."

"What a nice thing to say. Thank you."

"Why did you marry him in the first place?"

"Do you really want to know? It will sound crazy, but I thought he was opening new worlds to me. He introduced me to crime fiction, to Ross MacDonald, Ed McBain, Michael Connelly..."

"That is so fucked up," Elsie said, stamping out her cigarette. "By the way, Jack's got everyone smoking like it was America in the nineteen-sixties. I'm a yoga mat girl, this simply won't do."

"I'm not ready to stop yet. I'm looking for a reason."

"What do you think of Hawk?" she asked. Then without waiting for an answer, she barreled ahead. "He tried hitting on me, how clueless. I don't go that way. I think you already know that."

"I have never been in love," I said.

"I'm different than you," she said. "I only love deeply."

Elsie was not like anyone I had ever met before. She seemed to know where I was, finding those places I always worked to keep hidden, before even I did.

"You're sleeping with Jack," she said, stating it almost as if it was a question. "Don't get me wrong, my brother is the sweetest of the sweet, but you should know that Azalea will be joining us tonight. They spend time together, if you know what I mean."

"I'm not sure Jack has mentioned her," I said, keeping calm and only wondering why Jack had not told me when we were playing at honesty earlier.

"She's an actress on the show. How are you feeling now that you know this?"

"Like the fool I always seem to feel like. But I'll get over it. You can get over anything, trust me on that."

She reached across the space between our chaises and squeezed my hand. "Scotty, I'm glad you're here," she said, these simple words no different than if she had looked devotedly into my eyes and said, Scotty, I will be here for you always.

The evening was a fast montage, more chardonnay, catered vegan, a DJ spinning music, not a song I would ever recognize, meeting all these new people, all of them in the industry, all of them talking a new language to me, showrunners and script editors and executive producers, all of them arrogantly young and talented and seemingly unaware of their good fortune. I had made it to Los Angeles at last.

It all ended outside under the stars, as we settled in for a viewing of new episodes of Jack and Elsie's series. A crazy-large projection screen rose out of the slate decking, don't ask me how, motorized and retractable, and newfangled headsets were passed out to each of us. We looked like rich space martians with our glasses of wine, nibbling from cheese and dessert boards, watching Jack Kerouac tower over the glittering city like Godzilla.

Before I tell you more, I should mention that Jack's on-and-off-screen interest, Azalea, was an astonishing and flawless beauty. My eyes went to her often this evening, there was no way to compete with that, not that I wanted to exactly. I was sorry that Jack had not confided in me about her, leaving me to feel in that lonely left-out way—*what did I do to deserve this*? But I did not know how to get angry with Jack, he was a charming sweet chivalrous man-child, and like the iconic novelist he played on TV, he didn't seem always capable of handling the mundanities that make up the day-to-day. I found him easy to forgive, I knew he meant well, which is more than most people, trust me, you will all learn that.

Now I don't know if I could be this magnanimous if Elsie had not been doting on me, refilling my wine glass, fetching me a sweater and blanket for the night air before ever being asked, smiling at me and making contact when I would otherwise be startlingly alone. I guess the real question is how forgiving of Jack would I be if I knew, what I would later know and which would inform every detail to come, that there was a baby growing inside of me, his baby, of course.

I sat between Jack and Elsie, aware of the strangeness of being west, in a lonely sea of silhouetted guests, watching their show, this bright amazing flickering, mesmerized by the quality of their art, really truly, they were artists and they had my utmost respect.

Jack, though he might be a second-rate novelist, was a magnificent actor. He brought me in, held me, captivated me in a way that he could not ever do in this other realer life. He *was* Jack Kerouac.

I was also staggered by the depth of Elsie's scripts. She had told me that she had studied literature at Harvard like me, just a decade earlier, and had followed that with USC Film School. But nothing could prepare me for the ambition and stark genius of a writer who knows what she wants to do and who delivers it, never imagining for a quivering instant that the arrow will not pierce the bullseye.

I loved Jack and I loved Elsie, and I loved being in the house that my dead mother once shared with her lover, their father. I went to asleep alone that night though, I want to be clear about that, because I was just beginning to figure myself out.

Chapter 19

I reclined by the pool in a borrowed swimsuit and burrowed my way into the novels of Jack Kerouac. The hot dry winds picked up about midday. But I was determined to read my way through. Elsie checked on me periodically, bringing out sun lotion, scrambled egg whites, and multiple lattes, and I continued bravely on, wanting really very much to begin to love Kerouac. Mind you, I saw what an American original he was, Dalton was right, every sentence and every absent comma was inimitably indelibly Kerouac, but truthfully it was not for me, and I was made sad by the lifestyle of he and his Beat friends, one long nameless stretch of beery turnpike, sometimes a pretty mountain or two, an endless wandering in the moment, a never finding, a sordid cocktail of drink sex jazz and Catholic zen, I know I had no right to talk, since I was on my own road to nowhere, but this is where I was with all of it, thought you'd want to know.

I interrupted my dedicated excursion into Kerouac land only for my weekly scheduled meeting with Dorian and Cage's senior management team, which included the COO, Wendell Sammeler, the CFO, Melissa Albright, and head of legal, Crane Wetland. Obviously I didn't want them to know I was poolside on the in-house video conference call, so I put a blouse over my bikini top and borrowed Elsie's sunglasses, and made sure the video frame showed little else but the dreary brown canyon backdrop.

They wanted to know what I was thinking, of course, and of

course I knew already what they were thinking. I was careful not to say much, just the usual, We're exploring every option, We should look into that, Interesting idea, that kind of thing, I let them do the squirming and I let them fill in my willful silences. They wanted to know if I was selling, and if I was selling was I selling all of it or just Martin Cage's half of the concern. I could see where that would matter to them, because if I sold all of it, then we would in all likelihood be swallowed by one of the Big Five, and that meant their services might no longer be necessary, that they might become redundant, collateral damage.

Melissa suggested that we might lay off some of the senior staff to show how serious we are about cost cutting. Wendell chimed in that was a brilliant move on the chessboard. Now I knew that Melissa and Wendell had rehearsed this dialogue, and I also knew they didn't really care about cost cutting—but certainly they did care how they might appear under the scrutiny of a new owner.

The higher up you got on the food chain the more you understood that the official truth was really the official lie. Self interest and greed, and this has been my experience as a chief executive, were always what lay behind every decision. What really went on in the back rooms and executive suites and the boardrooms of this country was only how to make these selfish, myopic decisions look palpable to the average fool.

We are born liars. There is not anything we do that does not seem to be the sperm and the egg of a lie. Even when we hand out our rejection slips to the agents and their strangely mortified authors, refusing them entry into the club, there is little truth. If we say to you that your writing is "energetic," what we are really saying is that it is all over the place, a mess of energy. If we say that you are rich at character development, then we are really saying that your novel is a snooze-fest. If I tell you that we might be interested to take another look at the book if certain issues are addressed, that if you give another six months of rewriting to this ongoing tragedy, then what I'm saying to you is, Won't you please go away already?

Everything is code. Sometimes we are polite in our rejections, not because someone has written a fine book but because the agent is powerful and we want another book from another author on his or her list. It is rare that we really have the chance as a publisher to say what we feel and mean. I would love to write the rejection letter that begins with, *Are you out of your fucking mind?*

One of the things I've always admired about Sully Sullivan, for example, is that he has over three-hundred different form letters for rejection, and he's smart enough to keep the rinse cycle going from agent to agent, none of them keying in on his deception, all of them thinking, what a fine gentleman Sully is, taking the time to consider the novel and to comment back on it in an original, hard-fought way.

And let me bring you all in on another little industry secret. Many literary agents and editors don't actually even read books. They have readers who do that sort of dreaded thing. Readers are the bottom dwellers—to move up the ranks they have to read read read and then perhaps discover in those slushy piles something worth reading, and then if the reader discovers enough, he or she gets to climb another slippery rung, and then maybe someday, too, gets to a point where reading isn't necessary anymore, such heaven. These are the ghost readers at the big publishers and agencies, kept out of sight, in back rooms, their skin sallow and pasty from all their time under the fluorescents, like graduate students pulling an endless succession of all-nighters, you can spot them right away, the way their mole-like eyes squeeze to adjust to daylight, the way they live on coffee and vending machine treats, their whole presence teeming with the apologetic, a verging on indentured servitude.

After the video conference I returned to my Kerouac, proudly a reader again myself. One thing I need to say right now is that I know the distance of my privileged Upper East Side upbringing to Kerouac's brave blue-collar wanderings—and I thought how he would deal with such ludicrous video management calls and how I might do in his hardscrabble position, hoboing the country with a knapsack, and I decided that we would both be terrible at being each other.

Smoky fires erupted in the nearby hills late in the afternoon. Elsie told me not to worry, that this happened often enough. Santa Ana winds, she said, were the real concern. Helicopters inked the dark skies like locusts, dumping retardant on the orange flames. The winds continued to pick up, and large palm fronds fell like wooden leaves. And by the time the pomegranates were dropping near me, smashing to the decking, their pulp staining like red blood, I gathered my books and headed back into the house.

We need to talk about sex now, there is just no getting around it, unfortunately. I don't want to titillate, I don't want to describe Elsie and I in our swimsuits, the way it was, yes, alone in the house, Jack somewhere else doing reshoots, uncorking more chardonnay, dancing together to synthetic music in the living room, the apocalyptic fires glowing from every window—but there you have it.

Before all that, though, she shared with me the book she is writing. The show was done for the season, and Elsie had first thought she was going to write a play with the small opening in her schedule. But the play turned into a novel, and the portion of the novel she showed me was so good that it scared me, scared me that it couldn't continue to be this good, yet it was, and it continued to be, bringing me to my knees, yes, sexually and literally, don't be shocked, how unnecessary, this is the world we live in now, please just get over it.

Jack had slept with a hundred-and-fifty humans. Who knew, perhaps that was even on the low side for a television star. Stuart, still legally my husband, was bisexual or something like it. He had slept with Susan Ogden, as both a man and as a woman, that much now seemed certain, and he was currently having sex with Kent. He used to sleep with me—but here's the rub, how could I seethe or complain, I have always been elsewhere, the stories emanating from my abused and pornographic mind seeded with rape and lesbian submission, so difficult for the traditionalist in me, all of it too debased and scatological, for it is the lyrical that moves me in fiction, why, the reason I read books in the first place, to leave my own story behind.

All those lovers, real and make believe, like the diversity in our novels, no longer are any of us belonging to any one genre, think of the daring Kerouac gathering his edgy, revolutionary material— code for the homoerotic overtones that are unmistakeable in all of his work—in the nineteen-forties, for heaven's sake, and here we are now, in another century, so I will not apologize for sleeping with Elsie and for finding my true voice.

Let us go back to Elsie's writing, which made me wet and gloriously wanting in the first place. Her novel, at least for the time being, was being called *Nat and Scott*. It was about the friendship of Nathaniel West and F. Scott Fitzgerald at the end of their lives, when both of these Great American Novelists were living on the edge of forgottenness, at the Garden of Allah Hotel on Sunset Boulevard, Nat writing *The Day of the Locust*, Scott toiling on *The Last Tycoon*, all between the hacked-out movie scripts that paid their bills, two of the best who would ever be, penning the two greatest Hollywood novels ever, smoking their cigarettes, drinking their drinks, wondering what had happened and why the good times had passed them by, for me you can not tell a more engrossing and moving story, and here was Elsie telling it.

Nat and Scott would die within hours of each other. F. Scott having his final heart attack just before Christmas in 1940, Nat rushing back with his wife from Mexico to pay his respects to his dear friend, running a stop sign in El Centro, dead everyone dead, the bodies of both novelists, independent of each other, mere coincidence, shipped in their caskets on the same railroad train East, crossing a country of suddenly deceased possibility, the end of so so much if you care about books as I do.

As I said, Elsie could not tell me a more riveting bedtime story. I adored her writing, that always comes first for me, her words were like love sonnets, and then I loved her body, why not, and we fell into each other, a long late afternoon of that, and when we came out of the languor that followed our coitus, the fires were still burning in the hills, but I was no longer afraid of anything.

Nat and Scott, Elsie and Scotty, Jack and me, all the books that need to be written, how few will be, this is true for all of our lives, everyone has great stories and most of them will never be told. I wished I could write like Elsie, though; if I were a novelist I would want to be just like her; is there a higher compliment?

We decided to have dinner out. We strolled down the winding hill, past the mini chateaus and pink villas, often holding hands, our eyes tearing up from the smoky haze, landing on Beachwood, a handsome, palm-treed avenue of aquamarine apartment complexes.

"What do you think is happening with us?" Elsie asked, as we continued to walk.

"It's impossible to think that I did not know you yesterday morning," I said.

We walked all the way down to the base of the hill, to a small commercial stretch on Franklin, where huge, snorting silver trucks were lined up like a wagon train. A movie crew had set up on the sidewalk, a congested scene of hot white light and orchestrated chaos, and as we detoured past, I craned my head to see if I might glimpse the stars behind the cordoned-off ropes. I noticed that Elsie never even bothered to glance in the direction of those insanely bright lights, it was clear this was a non-event in her world, no more unusual than a Tuesday street cleaning.

She steered me into a restaurant called La Poubelle that she insisted would ring my bells. It was dark and old-fashioned, white tablecloths and gilt-framed mirrors and ancient posters for French aperitifs, escargot and red wine and coq au vin, easy to pretend we were on the Left Bank, utterly perfect for our moment right now, dingaling.

After we were seated Elsie asked if I minded if she checked her phone messages, and I said I didn't, and I didn't, again this is the way the world is now. I tasted my cabernet and looked across the table at her with a feeling I had never experienced before, a mixture of sexual desire and unrepentant grief. I was grieving for the wasted years, the lost time that can never be called back. Fitzgerald died at the age of forty-four, Kerouac at forty-seven, and I wondered if at the moment of their departures they grieved more for the loves they had yet to experience or for the books they did not get a chance to write.

When Elsie was done hearing her messages, she said, "Thank you, Scotty. I'm sorry for the intrusion. Forgive me for noticing, but I have yet to see you check your own phone since you arrived."

I took it out of my handbag. And I pressed a button to bring it out of its dormancy.

"You mean you've had it off this entire time?" Elsie said, disbelieving.

I placed the cell on the table between us. The sound of thirty-two unheard messages trilled, one after the other. I put it on speaker, as if this action proved that I would never lie to her.

The first message was from Jack. "Scotty, I'm so sorry I didn't tell you about Azalea. I don't want this to come between us. Call me."

Actually, the next four messages were from Jack and they offered a similar sentiment.

"I will talk to Jack," Elsie said. "I know how to handle this."

"Let's just tell him the truth," I said. "Life is infinitely easier that way."

Sadie called next. She said, "Just wanted to see how you were doing and that you are okay. All is well on the home front. Dalton continues to type like a madman. Georgie is still here, oh God, when will she ever leave, that's a whole other story. I'm glad you made it to California. Miss you tons, darling girl. You were right, I should have come with you."

Georgie had called, too. "Hey sister, Stuart is forging contracts for his dead authors. Call me. Oh and by the way, love your apartment. Could get used to living this way."

Dalton followed Georgie, which seemed fitting. "Dust off the

National Book Award and Pulitzer Number Two," he said. "I'm in the home stretch."

I could tell Elsie was surprised by my openness, which was its own largesse, but she went with it and didn't say much, just looked across at me with the curiosity of a new love, trying I'm sure to understand why I would want to be so unedited and undistilled. Is there any greater intimacy than letting someone see our sentences before we meld and anvil them through the traditional style guide?

Leyton sounded somber, and I knew I was unprepared for what he had to say. "Scotty, I hate to leave this as a message," he said, and already from his tone, it would be bad, only a question of degree. I hit the pause button and poured some more cab in each of our glasses.

"You don't have to do this," Elsie said.

"I do, though," I said. "I want not even a smidgen of dishonesty between us. My father used to say, We're only as sick as our lies. The beginning of every novel, the first sentences and paragraphs, tells us everything we will ever need to know."

I hit play. Leyton said, "Sully Sullivan died last night, looks like a heart attack, at least natural causes of some sort, I mean he was in his early eighties. So sorry, know how much he has meant to you and your father. There's more, unfortunately, Scotty. Wish it wasn't so. There's another death in the family. We need to get you home as soon as possible. Hendricks, this will make the papers in the morning, plowed his Jaguar into the Apple store, mistook the brake pedal it seems for the gas. Fortunately, nobody else was killed. But the Crop Duster is no more. *The Daily News* has a gruesome photo of him smashed into a display of iPads and Macs, you are forewarned. So sorry, Scotty, call me when you can."

I gasped twice in the course of Leyton's message, at the obvious plot points, and then I began to tear up, thinking about these two ancient high priests of our firm, who had given their lives in holy pursuit of literature, as if only the books, which were our sacraments, would ever matter—were we all so fucking crazy to have given so much and loved so hard, to have this ineffable faith?

The deaths of Sully and Hendricks, following so close to Marty's passing, were like an exclamation point after the manuscript words The End!, as if subtlety was forever lost and it had to be drummed into all of us that the sublime first-edition world we had once celebrated and held so dear was now on the remainder table, priced down and cheapened, the author's names stamped over with cash register reductions.

Poor Sully, poor Hendricks, poor all of us.

I told Elsie I probably had only another day before I would I have to head back to New York, to deliver eulogies at Campbell's, and she looked stricken and deathly sad, and I'm sorry to say that pleased me, because I liked her, too.

After dinner we browsed the used bookshop that was next door to La Poubelle. I was studying the titles on a long shelf of Larry McMurtry in the M-S aisle, remembering how much I enjoyed *Lonesome Dove* one summer long ago and reflecting why I never read another book of his, and there were so many he had written in his career, memoirs and novels, and I was checking out the jacket copy of *Buffalo Girls*, thinking I'd get that and maybe another one, too, maybe *Somebody's Darling*, I had never heard of that one, and wondering if McMurtry was still alive, and if he was, how old was he, and what was the last thing he published, when Elsie called over to me.

"Hey, Scotty Legs, how do you feel about Irwin Shaw?" she asked. "I just found first editions of *Evening in Byzantium* and *Lucy Crown*."

Before I could share her excitement, Elsie said, "I think he's pretty great, really underrated. He may be one of the best ever, actually. *The Young Lions* is one of my all-time favorites."

Chapter 20

I just kept trying to answer the one question I'm always trying to answer, which is, What am I doing, what am doing with my life, am I out of my mind, what am I doing, am I absolutely insane? What is this life we are living, who are we? This is what I was asking myself as I hurriedly repacked my bag for travel back to New York. Only moments before I had been on the phone with a reservations clerk, and if I hurried—and I was hurrying, the Uber was on the way—I'd make a flight out of Burbank leaving in less than two hours.

I rose early this morning, and in the softness of dawn, in what is usually a meditative space for me, where I often can make sense of the day ahead, my thoughts soon became my enemies, all frantic and unswerving, taking me over a mental cliff. An old, familiar fear was back, clammy and inescapable, and we'll come back to that, but first I need to talk about Elsie and my feelings there.

I was drenched with the guilt of furtive, improper sex, there, even saying that is quite difficult for me, I had been with a woman for the first time, not just anyone but the woman of my careful dreams, which is really the difference between fantasizing about something for years and a physical reality you don't finally believe will ever happen, the odd disconnect between hidden thoughts and a warm mouth and tongue, and yes, I must say it, her Lolita loins, her smell still on me, oh, how much I liked it, finally someone who didn't maul my breasts, the knowing of another she, my virginity at last taken, it didn't matter that I was married and had been with a few men, I was changed in the way of the caterpillar to the butterfly. But now I was desperate to flutter away, surely you understand that, each new turn pushing us forward, winged or not, it all arrives at a lone death.

There's more, there's always more. When we arrived home last night, there was a canary-yellow Hummer parked close to the house, facing downhill, its occupant quite noticeable, the driver-side window down, his chubby hand gripping a nubby cigar, a Stetson crowning his hammy head, at first Elsie thought—she would tell me this later—that it was an encamped photographer, they were used to that sort of thing, sometimes these celebrity stalkers would be out there for days and nights on end, ghost detectives as empty as the Starbucks cups and In-N-Out wrappers lying at their feet.

"Evening, ladies," the stranger drawled into the nighttime quiet, as Elsie moved quickly to unlock the front gate. "Got a message for you, Miss Dorian, from an intimate relation who will remain nameless at this juncture for reasons that you yourself have initiated. The fat lady ain't sung yet. This ain't over, it ain't even begun, get used to your privacy being interrupted, lady. Now you enjoy the rest of your evening, you hear."

I don't know how I found it in myself, but I strolled right up to his open window, only a couple of feet from the smelly smoke rising from his nubby cigar, my heart jackhammering adrenalized fear. Somehow, though, I managed some psycho intensity of my own and said, "You can relay a message to your client. Tell him he's dead to me, dead in every single way, dead dead dead."

I backed away and walked through the gate, not showing a card, as unblinking as if I was at the final table of the World Series of Poker—but you can well imagine how creeped out and shaken I was, it took a solid hour on the couch with Elsie's soothing attentions to calm me down. Actually, I didn't so much calm down as it all somehow led to another frenzied bout of sex, the sense of shared danger connected to so much else, I felt so teary-eyed alive and wanting to prove it, and Elsie went with me, though I could tell she was ill at ease with what was driving me.

After it was over Elsie said, "I didn't like that, Scotty. I felt like I could've been anybody to you, just a body, do you know what I mean."

Of course I was sure the Stetson-hatted messenger had been sent by Stuart, not that I could prove it. I reported it to Leyton first thing, not that he could do anything about it. Hawk had checked this morning, and the driver and his Hummer were still there, but Hawk had the good sense to take a photo of the license plate, which I sent on to Georgie Guns. Soon after the Hummer was gone, even if my helter-skelter thoughts remained.

There was so much to think about. I had disappointed Elsie with my soulless, determined humping. There was a creep in a cowboy hat following me. Lizza was in a mental hospital, still being evaluated. Yes, Lizza, I kept coming back to her, it wasn't just that two of our senior editors had died yesterday and how much we needed her seasoned guidance as a publicist right now, not just with the media and the preparations for their services at Campbell's, or that I just missed having a trusted lieutenant to advise me. But it was that Lizza was so much braver than I knew how to be. I recalled her marriage ceremony on Nantucket, I was with Stuart, and somehow without any full articulation of this I knew from watching her embarking on happiness with Mara that I was truly lost at sea, that I was sleeping with a sociopathic stranger in a place called the Driftwood Motel, the taste of brine embedded in our skin and clothes, he did not even notice my salty tears as we went to bed that night, me in ivory lace, untouched and alone, the things that stay with us.

Sully Sullivan had also been alone. He had been married only briefly as a young man for a few years or so. What of all the other decades? Who kissed his long neck and forehead and whispered don't let the bedbugs bite? Hendricks had been in a long-standing marriage of a half century or more, but I also knew they slept in separate bedrooms in their Park Avenue apartment, passing each other in the long hallways like polite but distant phantoms, maybe he just hit the gas pedal on purpose and said, Why not, why the hell not, if it's all the same to you?

I have just reread that last paragraph, and it strikes me that I used the word "long" three times, and I think the reason why is that it is part of longing, and that is what all of us shared, a longing for love, yes, certainly that, but also a longing for the way things used to be in our business, that imagined golden glow of a better time.

I didn't want to sell Dorian and Cage, it's all I had, it belonged to all of us, to my father and brother, to my dearest friend Marty, it was every memory, every belief, every everything. I frantically, because everything was frantic today, searched my Rolodex mind for a rich human who might care about the future of books and the future of me. Our nada who art in nada, nada be thy name thy kingdom nada thy will be nada in nada as it is in nada, as our friend Mr. Hemingway said so well.

My phone made that funny little sound—the Uber was out front, waiting. And that's when Elsie and Jack appeared at my door together, just as I picked up my bag and was ready to abscond.

Jack said, "I know everything. Don't leave. There's more to talk about. Whole books yet to be written, you know it."

Elsie said, "Scotty, were you not even going to say goodbye?"

Jack said, "You've been with both of us. There, I said it, it's out in the open."

Elsie said, "I think I love you, Scotty. There, I said it."

Jack said, "That makes sense. Not everything does. But you and Elsie make sense."

At that moment I wanted to collapse to the floor and be committed to the nearest psychiatric institution, how nice to be wheeled in an ancient wooden chair, shivering in the heat, a nurse saying, there, there, don't you worry about a thing, Scotty, it is all a dream, a very believable and persuasive dream, would you like me to read to you, perhaps Faukner's *As I Lay Dying*, we haven't read that one recently, would that make you happy, Scotty dear?

At that moment we heard from the living room below a clear, loud voice that said, "I'm home! Is anyone else up and about?"

We heard him coming up the stairs, the strange apprehension of what he meant to each of us, of course I knew it was Jack and Elsie's dad, Shane Gregory, my mother's lover and the one she left us for.

In seconds he was standing before us, a tall, lean, beautiful man in his early sixties, his still-thick hair a rugged gray, this virile man who stood on surf boards and curled his way through the waves of life, and my first thoughts were sexual, shame on me, seeing exactly what my mother had seen in him, which was so obvious, the opposite of my portly father, but also thinking even in the hundred-year span of a second, that, yes, he looked extremely fuckable even now and surely then. When would it ever stop, I had already been with both Jack and Elsie, and I knew that I had missed my Uber ride and my plane out of here, what would happen next, and did it really matter, you tell me, your turn now.

Chapter 21

Shane Gregory and I sat with a bottle of Vinho Verde—a tart, crisp, green-apple-tasting white from a favorite vineyard of his in Portugal; he casually invited me to accompany him there someday—between us at one of the poolside tables, candles flickering in the blue evening, the burnt smell of the fires still with us, it was romantic whether either of us would ever admit to that or not, while his two children watched down on us with trepidation from one of the many balconies of the mansion.

We had had dinner as a family. Shane is an excellent cook, and he made simple things that were deliciously complex, gluten-free rice fettuccine with the the best pesto I have ever sampled, a red-leaf spinach salad with a ginger tahini dressing, sensationally topped off by wild, fist-size sea scallops, marinated in wine and garlic oil and seared to translucent perfection on the gas grill. He made it look easy, as easy as his life must appear from any outsider's perspective, if you did not know differently and know that he had lost his two great loves, one to an accidental overdose, another drowned in a pool, which seemed like another overdose of some kind, the patterns that make up a life, was it destiny or happenstance, unchosen or perhaps chosen in ways that baffle our best intended selves, I'll leave that to Dr. Jung and his ilk to decide.

Dinner was polite, Shane talked about the surf conditions he had experienced, a new language for me of big waves and sets and breaks and cutbacks and nose-dives, Jack and Elsie regaled him with tales from their business of making a show, much of it financial, viewer numbers and residuals, some of it common and gossipy, hookups among cast and crew, and I stayed quiet and neutral, taking it all in like a goldfish in a bowl peering out at the strange, other-worldly universe just beyond the glass, the ordinary living room that could pass for Mars.

At some point in all of this politeness, he said impolitely, "I'm sorry, Elsie and Jack, but I need to talk to Scotty alone. I hope you won't mind, but even if you do, it's just the way it will be."

I looked boldly now into Shane's algae green eyes, that spoke to all the depths and years, I wanted so to know and to understand how it all happened, how my mother left us for him, I mean, in one way it was easy to see and all, Shane himself was like a titanic ocean wave, if he took you under you might never come up for air again.

"There's a lot you don't know," he said. "I hoped one day we'd be here, but what are the odds of that? Anyway, what's your email, and please don't you dare resist?"

I gave it to him of course, and he tapped it into his phone and then said, "I just sent you all the letters and photos between your mother and myself. I've also included the novel she was writing when she died. And then, and this will be hard for you, I also sent you an hour of your mother talking, and she is really speaking to you and Bumby shortly before she died. She loved you crazily both so much, and I filmed her back in the day, must be the early eighties, with one of the first video recorders, an enormous dino of a thing. But I've transferred the tape to digital and now you have it, I hope it might help, we'll see, you'll let me know."

I had to look away from him for a moment and out towards the dark canyon, to give myself room, I found him unnerving, too all seeing, too true to be good, maybe. He poured me some more wine in the off moment, waiting for me to return.

Shane said, "I'm not sure how far to take this, but I think, now that your father is gone, that I should tell you more of the truth—

are you ready for it, that's the real question?"

I nodded and tilted back more wine like it might help. He said, "Your father was no saint. How are you feeling even as I suggest this?"

I nodded and drank some more. "He was never faithful to your mother, believe me on this, I don't think you know that. I wish I didn't have to be the one to tell you. But when I met her she was unhappy and very much suffering alone. She was no harlot, as your father in all likelihood made her out to be. I will not lie to you, you are the daughter of the one person I loved in this life."

"My father could never even speak her name after she left," I said.

"He was seeing someone else, and it broke your mother's heart. Excuse me now."

He left me there for a few minutes, by the still pool, left to contemplate my father's infidelities and all that has ever shaped me. Jack and Elsie were still above me, pouring their own wine, and trying to imagine the conversation their father might be having with me.

Shane returned with another bottle of Vinho Verde. He also gripped something else in the other hand—a gold statuette. He passed it over to me, an Oscar engraved with his name and the year of his win for Best Original Screenplay.

"I owe that as much to your mother, as anyone," he said, watching me study it. "I was with her when I was writing it. We used to read to each other at night, she from her novel, me from the damn script. Books and scripts are only as good as the times you are living in. We were having fun, that's why it was so doubly awful what happened."

He poured some more wine, and he said, "Here comes the hard part, Scotty. I need for you to hear something that will probably hurt. But I'm going to ask anyway—do you want to hear it?"

I looked again into the algae green eyes of my mother's lover, this eternal surfer, wondering where all this was going, but you can't brace yourself for hurt, anyway, it just will be, no different than waves, I imagine, one after the other, you can only prepare so much, paddling out, working hard not to overthink, life's ocean so much bigger than all of us, just lift yourself up from the board, get a good grip, here we go, here we go, don't ever look back, it's the unknown after all that we seek, steady steady steady, let it wash over us.

"Scotty," he delivered, "your mother did not accidentally overdose. It was a suicide. Your father knew that, too—he made sure that the truth was buried. She took the pills intentionally. And it was all because she had let you and Bumby down. She couldn't live without you—and she knew your father would never let her regain custody."

I can handle this, I thought, I can handle this wave, it is what it is...

Then this: "There's something else that needs to be said, and I wish it had been said earlier, in case what I tell you becomes more problematic than we both would ever have wanted. I really don't know the situation with you and Jack and Elsie. I mean, I knew Jack was writing a book and wanted you to see it. But even he doesn't know what I'm about to say.

"Here goes nothing: I may be your biological father, I may not be, but there is a distinct possibility. Elsie and I were never really sure, we had been together at that time, tests were never done, and who knew we would ever be here, as you can well guess."

Wiped out, crashing to the ocean floor, swirling under the currents of white, opening my eyes to the salt and the sand, I can't breathe, I'm not sure I even want to come up for air, I'll just be hit by another gargantuan wave, what's the point, I'm not that strong, and if I die down here it might be better, what's one more drowning in a family used to them.

Chapter 22

It was a game of quantum roulette, as I was left to contemplate landing in the worst possible universe, no different than a bullet to the head. I won't hold you in odd suspense, Shane Gregory is not my biological father, what an incurable nightmare if he had been, then I would have been sleeping with my half-sister and half-brother, gladly I will not be making that particular confessional call to Leyton Smulders.

There was a tiny piece of me, perhaps it wasn't even all that tiny, and this is not to shrug off the horror of what would have been, understandably enough, accidental incest, that wanted to have a father who was still very much alive and to be a part of a family again.

Thankfully we did not have to wait long to do the tests and receive the results. The rich and famous do not live like you do—yes, they certainly have more money, as Hem said to Fitz, but they also have far better connections. When a deep-tissue massage or an ounce of Blue Hawaiian is desired, it is the ease of home delivery, no different than ordering a pizza, and so it was with the blood work. Jack made a call—yes, the whole family was involved now.

A young, bearded man, ostensibly a doctor named Saul, appeared at the door an hour later, it was late, almost midnight. He had pulled up in a sleek silver van that he told us worked as a mobile laboratory. He stuck a clean needle into Shane and I, took his samples, said he'd know the results shortly.

Of course there was a hitch, why are you not surprised. After delivering the good news, Saul asked me to have a private word with him, and I accompanied him back out to his van, out of the family's earshot.

"Here's the thing, señorita," he said, stroking his beard, as if debating how to tell me whatever it was that required secrecy, "and I don't mean to be invasive. This isn't my business, but maybe you don't know and I think you'd probably want to know."

I was listening intently, but I also couldn't help noticing the yellow Hummer parked across the street, back again. The windows were rolled up and I couldn't tell if the creep in the Stetson was behind the black glass.

"Your blood shows a hormone called human chorionic gonadotrophin," Saul continued, "hCG for short. Here's the thing, you're pregnant. I'm guessing only a short time by the hormone levels. Hope it's all good news. Listen, I've got to scram, I'm due somewhere else. Good meeting you."

As I watched Saul get into the van, as I vaguely wondered about his next strange delivery, my mind raced to recall when I ovulated last so that I could calculate to the day how long I might be pregnant with Jack's child.

Chapter 23

My father bought the cedar-shingled traditional that was built in 1913, along with its accompanying guest cottage, all of it resting on a grassy acre in East Hampton, for less than a hundred thousand dollars, of course that was the purchase price in 1968, well before the Wall Street barons and tech lords helicoptered into town, erecting their turreted castles and twenty-bedroom getaway cottages, the potato fields transformed into landing strips and gunite swimming pools, making it all just a little bit more miserable for the writers and editors and artists in the colony, who my father like to call the original settlers and who were never that happy a lot to begin with, anyway.

As a young girl I loved our family times at the summer house. Bumby and I spent the long, sun-glistened days biking around, pedaling to the ocean beaches or into town for ice cream or to the community tennis courts, never bothering to update our ancient wood racquets, or our bikes for that matter, which were old, reliable Schwinns. We were crazy for lawn games—badminton, croquet, and bocce ball—joining our father and his friends, who participated with their customary handicap, one hand always lost to a vodka and soda or an ashed-down cigarette.

I bring all of this up because East Hampton is where we have landed, it's complicated, of course, like everything that I seem to touch these days. We flew back to New York early morning by private jet, Jack had insisted. And by saying we I mean Elsie,

Hawk, and I.

I didn't keep the news of the pregnancy from Jack, or from Elsie, either. We were all in this together now, whether I wished it or not. Jack not only gallantly arranged for the jet, he also made sure that Hawk accompanied us, he was concerned for my safety after the second sighting of the Hummer.

I told them I was worried about my advancing age, and that I wanted to consult an obstetrician as soon as possible. Jack asked if I wanted to keep the baby. I asked him what he wanted, isn't this the conversation men and women have been having from the beginning of time. And here's what he had to say: "Scotty, I'm a Catholic and as a Catholic I don't believe in abortion."

Elsie said, "Jack, you're not Catholic. We're Presbyterians."

Jack said, "Well, Jack Kerouac is Catholic."

"Oh my God," she said. "You're a lunatic."

Once we landed in New York, Hawk took us in the Range Rover to 1040 Fifth Avenue—oh before I continue, let me add that private jet is so the way to travel, even better if it is a Gulfstream owned by an entertainment conglomerate, soft leather seats the size of couches, an open bar and a menu selection that frankly would be hard to rival in even the best restaurant, oh, complete with an on-board chef, of course, which is not to leave out an honest-to-god bright and friendly air hostess-slash-actress, so talented that I actually believed she genuinely cared about our comfort and welfare, a real future for this one, I thought multiple times in our streak across the skies.

The best part was being next to Elsie, how a new love makes what was once onerous, the lost hours of air travel, bright and anticipatory. I just liked looking at her, inches away from me, her somehow poreless skin, no need for makeup, the press of her breasts against a simple cotton t-shirt, the eyes that were the same as Jack's, I had been perplexed about finding the perfect description for that color, I had made the mistake of calling it a Windex blue but that doesn't do her justice, I've seen that color in

Tiffany gemstones, Tanzanite and Helenite, close to aquamarine and topaz, but not quite, it's as if all of them were crystalizing together somehow to form the most dazzling eyes I have ever seen, how lucky I felt to be with her, what a savage and primal pleasure to be in her blue light.

I did not partake in the champagne, and more than once I had to wipe out the disquieting thought of fetal alcohol syndrome, you know the month I've had. Elsie brought herself close to me and told me not to worry so much, which is something I needed hearing, sometimes it's the simplest kindness that will get you thinking right again.

Hawk stayed to himself in the back of the plane, busied with a new author, Joan Didion's husband John Gregory Dunne, who had died more than a decade ago, Hawk was enthralled with the novel *Nothing Lost*, which was published posthumously—and I also noted a paperback version of *True Confessions*, next to him and next on his voracious assembly line.

I supposed Hawk would discover the novels of Dominick Dunne, John Gregory's brother, soon after. I did not know or ever get to meet the Dunnes, which is something to say in my world, but I admired them from afar, there was great tragedy and great writing in their family, something I could very much relate to. I've always been especially moved by the story of Joan Didion and John Gregory Dunne, husband and wife, writers working and living together, working alone together, separately publishing memoirs and novels, but sharing their works in progress with each other, creating screenplays together, living a doubly bi-lined life.

All I had to say to Elsie was, "Joan Didion and John Gregory Dunne."

"Dashiell Hammett and Lillian Hellman," she replied.

"Edmund Wilson and Mary McCarthy," I said.

"Good one, Scotty. How about Mary Shelley and Percy Shelley."

"Silvia Plath and Ted Hughes."

"Allen Ginsberg and Peter Orlovsky," she said. "And I'll throw in Anais Nin and Henry Miller for good measure."

"Louise Erdrich and Michael Dorris," I said, instantly regretting it.

"Oh, God, Scotty, that's awful. Dorris is the one who wrote that book about fetal alcohol syndrome. What was it called?—*The Broken Chord*? And wasn't he a suicide and didn't his kids accuse him of abuse?"

"Moving on, David Foster Wallace and Mary Karr," I said, only making things worse.

"How about a literary couple without a suicide in it?" Elsie said, laughing.

"Scotty Dorian and Elsie Gregory," I returned.

That's when she kissed me. Nice to be able to kiss on a plane, to just be. She was the best kisser I had ever known, that is not a small thing, I think. I was so glad that I invited Elsie to come east with me—yes, I asked her, I made that decision, I owned my feelings for once, how about that.

"Nobody likes a rich girl," I told Elsie after our lips parted. "People have always put up with me because there was all that tragedy in my family. The suicides made me more palpable."

"But I'm a rich girl, too," she said.

"But you lost your mother, that softens all of us."

"I see your point," Elsie said. "I mean, when I write characters I'm always looking to give them a tragic backstory. Otherwise most of us are just so unlikeable. I mean, look at us on this private jet, all this extravagant privilege, what viewer would dare take a hankering to us."

"I know, I have this Cambodian author, for example, I just acquired his memoir. He was taken hostage at the age of eleven and he winds up captive on this Thai fishing boat, as a reader you are rooting for him every page of the way, years and years of forced slavery at sea, the worst conditions imaginable, chained in an oily engine room, abused, beaten, one wrong move and you're dead, he watched other boys get their throats slit, that sort of thing, and somehow he perseveres and waits for his opportunity for escape, all or nothing. Now that's a book, that's somebody to root for."

"I think you're selling yourself short," Elsie said. "I'd root for you. I mean, you have a sociopathic husband who's hunting you down, you've just been impregnated by Jack Kerouac, you are embarking on your first gay love affair." Here she squeezed my hand reassuringly. "Then there's the fact that you are trying to save your company. You're looking desperately for a buyer. That sort of thing is appealing. I'd want to read more."

"What I need to do is murder Stuart, that's a real hook," I said. "That's when you really have something as an author. Murder is the great leveler in fiction."

I did not know it then, of course, deep in the plush leather of other class, but my husband would be murdered within the week, and it would not happen in any way that I could've imagined and plotted out.

As my reader I'm sure you've been wondering, perhaps even fretting, about all that. When was she going to come back to that? Are there enough pages left in the novel for Scotty to pull this off? It doesn't feel like there is the appropriate time allotted for the murder investigation and the subsequent trial, does it? Well, let me worry about that, that really is my job, if you think about it.

Have you also done the thing we all do, before we even begin to unpack a single sentence, and that is to count the total number of pages, to feel the heft or not-so-heft of the novel, beginning that simple accounting of how to pace yourself, as if the word count alone gave you a certain expectation of what was to come? And did you, after reading the opening line, to see if the book was worthy of a second sentence, fast forward to the last page and last paragraph and last sentence? Have you cheated on me, dear reader? If so, you know that I'm out of prison when this book ends.

Another off-putting thing many of the unfaithful will do is flip the book open to a random page, as if in this supreme power play, control can be shifted away from the author back to the reader—what outrageousness, to me that's just not adhering to that silent agreement we have with each other, the expectation that we will both play by the rules.

Now this is my story and I'll tell it the way I want to, of course you move forward with me at your own discretion, and I'll understand if you decide to bail for another title on your nightstand, but it is my hope that you will remain with me on this final stretch, and that my choices in these matters will, if not to your total liking, at least make a fair amount of sense to you, I do appreciate that you have stuck by me so far, it should be said—and everything should be said, don't you think.

Our East Hampton house is not on Lily Pond Lane, which is the most famous row of coveted properties, but it is within only a short walking distance of it, the soothing repetition of ocean waves can be heard on desultory nights through our windows and the air is forever scented with salt and the knowledge of stoic generations that came before us. My father bought the "six-bedroom sea cottage" from Sonny Weebler, who was the top editor of a fine publisher that no longer exists; when I consider it, I hope that is not the repeating pattern here, I hope I won't be selling soon either or not existing.

My father admired Sonny—Sonny had published a long list of impoverished Waspy writers, those Cheever types that went to good schools but whose families just pretended to be able to pay the bills—and he actually bought the house to help Sonny out of his own financial jam. It should also be noted that Sonny stayed with us in summers another ten years until his worn death, and his children and grandchildren are still always welcome at the house we call Crapshoot Manor, the phrase my father and Marty always used when publishing a novel by an unknown.

After we took possession of Crapshoot Manor, furnishings intact, we made only small, practical changes over the next unfurling half century of home ownership, upticks only to kitchen appliances, plumbing and cesspools, the heating and cooling systems, only the modernizing necessary not to be called a Luddite. My father refused to dig a pool or a tennis court, and he never seriously listened to the ever-present Hampton realtors who are and were always testing the waters, who brightly offer up that if you construct a greenhouse or a Swedish sauna or new landing pad that the value added is such and such, and so and so did it, as if home improvements were a kind of self improvement, a never-ending, never-doubting reflection of yourself.

We loved our home, and I love it still, outside it is a thousand shutters and dormer windows, those cedar shingles that will take on every outrageous and battering wind. Inside it is beadboard walls, wide-plank oak floors, and wood-beam ceilings. Inside again, there are the antique pine coffee tables, the Charles Stewart sofas and chairs in a sea blue, the clawfoot tubs in every bathroom, there are sunrooms with wicker furniture, fireplaces surrounded by bluestone tile, there are bentwood rockers, paintings of sea captains and angry waves done by Winslow Homer imitators, there are the cane-back armchairs, the art deco lamps, the lantern desk lamps from dead ships, the four-poster beds that have withstood a solid century, there is the crimson billiard table in the game room that my father added pockets to, I'm a solid shot you should know, there are party-serving bar carts as ubiquitous as salt shakers, and then the books, of course the books, in every room, shelf after shelf, a library with ladders on wheels to get to all those hard-to-reach high places, how great is that.

The appraiser, who came after my father died, warned me that if I was to sell I would have to rid the place of the books and even the shelves. He said that the modern buyer would be scared off by such a sight, why, no one has books anymore, he sniffed, even the emptied shelves were a flummoxing notion, what to do with such things.

When we arrived at Crapshoot Manor, the heat had been turned up and several of the fireplaces glowed with wood-crackling warmth. Sadie had called ahead to the caretaker, Lukas, who lived on the grounds in the guest cottage and watched over things for us. When my father was alive we changed caretakers every year—the idea was to gift the spot to a young, preferably penniless novelist who was in need of the time and space to write his or her masterpiece. Many of our caretakers did complete their novels and went on to become published, and of course that always felt good to us, nothing like the fat, self-satisfied glow of being generous to others.

Lukas, however, had been with us the longest, over three years now, he had been selected only a few months before Dad's final heart attack, and yet as far as I knew he was in the throes of a permanent case of writer's block. The young man who had first appeared to us fresh out of Iowa, neatly barbered and eager-faced, had grown a long, wintry Russian beard which, especially matched with his dark, sullen eyes, gave him the delusional appearance of a Raskolnikov, a look that pleaded with the world to see that he was so misunderstood, an extraordinary author forever on the verge, even though all anyone else could see was his obvious deterioration of mind.

The reason I had kept Lukas on was that Stuart detested him, was even frankly slightly afraid of him, which marvelously kept Stuart away from the premises. Stuart had tried to fire Lukas over a year ago, without telling me, and Lukas had been cagey enough to hold his ground and to telephone me.

I bring all of this up to say that Lukas was fiercely loyal to me, and that when we arrived at Crapshoot he asked to speak with me right away. He explained that Stuart had tried to break into the house just a few days earlier. Lukas, though, at the instruction of Leyton Smulders had changed all the locks. And when he came outside to confront the intruder, shotgun in hand, Stuart was challenged to explain himself.

"You know, he gave me a bunch of his usual flimsy excuses—look, I never liked the douche bag, not that that is some secret—saying that he had important papers he had to find and that kind of excuse shit, but I knew he wasn't supposed to be around here. I had the gun pointed right at him, and he thought better of the situation and backed the heck away. I could've shot him right then and there, totally justifiable, what a douche-bag bastard."

"I wish you had shot him," I told Lukas, and of course later I would wish I had never said such a thing.

"I know, sometimes you don't get second chances at something like this."

I moved quickly to change subjects. "Lukas, how's the writing coming along?"

"Slow," he said slowly, "real slow," and at that moment I had wished we had stayed on the subject of the justifiable homicide of my husband.

I excused myself, I had guests, after all. Dalton, Hawk, Elsie, Sadie, we had all just arrived in the Rover, I needed to help everyone settle in. Dalton was already organizing the expedition to dinner, he was in the expansive mood for aged, three-inch-thick steaks and five-pound lobsters, and he wanted to go to one of his old haunts, either The Palm or the Old Stove Pub or out to Montauk to Gurney's, there was going to be a vote and it was obviously one way or the other going to be a long, soppy evening, even if I was smartly abstaining.

I never did finish why we had left 1040 and decided to bail for the East End in the first place. When we arrived back at my apartment Dalton and Georgie were engaged in an epic row, screaming murderously at each other like something out of *Who's Afraid of Virginia Woolf*, Georgie even hurling a Chinese vase at Dalton's head, smashing it into a thousand pieces, each piece representing a ten-dollar bill.

"You fucking prick!" she screamed. "It's all about your penis, isn't it? You are nothing but a cock, you don't even have a brain, you probably even type with your penis!"

Then Georgie did the unforgivable, she grabbed a handful of Dalton's typed pages and slam-dunked them into the roaring fireplace. I am glad that Hawk was there to intercede at this moment, as we all saw the insane violence alight in Dalton's eyes, as he came rushing at Georgie like the college fullback he once was and Hawk tackled him to the carpet.

Georgie refused to calm down, refused to leave the premises, and that's how we came to be in East Hampton.

Chapter 24

The late autumn, red leaves blowing in the whipping winds, the howl of the ocean a forever seashell to our ears, biking with Elsie on the hedgy lanes, showing her my world, she has never been to the Hamptons, just as I had never been to Cali, mirrors upon mirrors, excited to park the Schwinns at a fish shack for lunch, just the two of us, off season, we are the only customers, not lonely at all, though, chardonnay for her and New England clam chowder for the both of us, her blue gemstone eyes swimming in my chocolatey eyes, warm and cozy in my L.L. Bean sweaters, thick and woolen—this time she is trying on my clothes.

Not that real life doesn't intrude. I started the morning on Skype with Leyton Smulders. He told me there wasn't much he could do about Stuart's unannounced visit to Crapshoot Manor. Stuart's attorneys have arranged for him to be at 1040 tomorrow afternoon to inventory his possessions. If all goes as intended, movers will arrive the following morning to remove everything that is not in dispute. Leyton believes I should be on the premises to oversee the sign-off on Stuart's inventory—of course, Leyton also advised that I bring a friend or even a bodyguard to make sure the transfer goes smoothly, and he volunteered to be there himself, if need be.

Now I told Leyton that I didn't know if I could stomach being in the same room as Stuart, and he further assured me that I did not have to have any face-to-face interaction with him, still I found the whole idea blood-curdling, almost inconceivable, the man is a well-heeled monster, most people cannot see what lies behind that J. Press exterior, they are unable to fully recognize his depravity and the danger he presents to others, all because of richly striped shirts and suits as silky as his triply-shaven face.

Stuart, whose legal bloodlust seems to only rival that of Scientologists and mega-wealthy megalomaniacs, had initiated yet another lawsuit, I am sadly getting used to seeing the word defendant as applied to me. The gist of it is that he was accusing Dorian and Cage of not living up to its contract with Kent, that our firm had not only not sufficiently publicized Kent's novel *The Fields of Play,* but that we have intentionally neglected it, as payback to Stuart, that I indeed let my personal animosity towards Stuart interfere with business as usual. Of course this was not true, and of course we would be able to prove it, eventually, but all nuisance suits were more than nuisances, they were coffer-draining exercises in futility, the only victors being the lawyering partners on both sides, not that Stuart cared, since these tiresome suits were being instigated and handled by one or more of his brothers, talk about personal.

It was true, though, that despite the fawning reviews of friendly critics (code for friends of the publisher and its authorial stable) and the expensive, decadent publicity— I'd just laid eyes on our bill from the Four Seasons launch party—that Kent's novel had sold few copies and seemed destined for the great remainder table in the sky.

All of this prompted me to ask Leyton how our counteroffensive was coming. Leyton informed me that he was exceedingly unhappy with Dr. Joyce Rock's interview. He had brought her into his office only yesterday to sculpt an affidavit for my countersuit against Stuart. Dr. Joyce is the key witness to his bullying, abusive behavior, since I only began therapy to deal with his dark narcissism and the absolute emotional distress it was causing me—and she, through her notes and memories of sessions, was capable of detailing the week-by-week state of my mind, which would clearly show that I was crazy afraid of Stuart and that we shared a deep suspicion he suffered from a classic case of narcissism, perhaps also borderline personality disorder, not that Dr. Joyce could diagnose any of this, because Stuart was not her patient, but she could nonetheless speak to my baseline fears, this was absolutely necessary testimony that we were counting on going forward.

Leyton told me, and this was quite a shock, really, that he considered Dr. Joyce a hostile witness at this point—and that he thought she would do more harm than good on the stand. He hesitated to give me details, which also concerned me greatly, and said that this was just one of those times where I needed to trust him.

There are things that will never be understood in this life, moments of disconnect with others, friendships that once seemed strong but which fall to the wayside, bonds severed for reasons that are never fully discerned, such was the case here with Dr. Joyce Rock. Strangely we would never speak again and our paths refused to cross. My calls and emails went unreturned, and never would I learn what I had done to spark her ire. Even though she did not honor her contract option with us for her next book, I did not chase her down a legal avenue, that nastiness is for others. Her Narc and Receptacle Series would be published by a competitor to great commercial success, and in the years to come, seeing an advertisement for her latest book or a critical review—the reviews are never polite when an author makes this kind of money—I would wonder all over again, for the life of me.

Following my call with Leyton, I also had another video conference with Dorian and Cage's senior management team. Sully Sullivan, in his last written instructions to his own attorney, had insisted on cremation and absolutely no funeral service whatsoever—I guess he wanted to spare others the pain of those doubleheaders that he was constantly attending, what a lovely fellow to the end. The service for the Crop Duster was tomorrow morning, though, and I would have to helicopter in with Dalton to say the usual few words. I had also instructed that our little publishing concern be closed for yet another week to appropriately mourn these fine editors and men, almost too much to bear, this accumulation, this on-going roster of death, this drawn-out ending to the book of our lives.

I also spoke to Georgie Guns, she was quite apologetic about her behavior in my apartment and offered to replace my smithereened vase, an offer which I should probably have accepted, but bygones be bygones had always been my father's motto, so let it be gone. Georgie also apologized for her extended stay and informed me that she was back in her Sutton Place pied-a-terre. Further good news, she had information about the canary-yellow Hummer and its Stetson-hatted owner. His name was Lee W. Heany, and he was indeed a private investigator working for Stuart. He was not exactly a first-class gentleman, according to Georgie and according to court records. Lee W. Heany had been accused multiple times of harassment, of conducting surveillance and of obtaining admissions through conduct unbecoming of a private dick, which is saying something, and in fact had had his PI license suspended twice after accusations of "dishonesty and fraud," yet still he operated, somehow immune to the laws that the rest of us are beholden to.

Georgie detailed Heany's last case. He was assigned, most basically, to harass a reality-show actress in Los Angeles, and his approach was really no different than writing her phone number in the bar's bathroom stall—you know, for a good time and a blowjob call Ginger at 555-and the other four digits—but Heany did all of this in cyberspace, and the results were exponentially more ludicrous and verged on lethal. He transposed the actress's face on porn advertisements—posting her real street address and apartment number and cell number—which promoted day-and-night three-ways and whatever action anyone might want. And they came knocking.

This is what I apparently had to look forward to. It gets worse—and doesn't it always. According to Georgie, Lee W. Heany had trailed me from California to New York. He had rented a Chevy Volt, red with New Jersey plates, at JFK shortly after we landed, and I had to suppose that he had by now sniffed us out in the Hamptons.

This was my morning, all before coffee.

But here I was now in the fish shack, eyes to eyes with Elsie, happy for all that had conspired to bring us together, to finally, miraculously, find the one person in the cosmic haystack who might be able save me from myself, for deep underneath all the smart trimmings and banter is a thought that never quite leaves me, one I haven't yet shared with Elsie, a sort of daily *un*-affirmation that goes like this: *I know the way out, if it all gets too hard for me, I know the way out.*

You see, I have always pondered the alternative to life, an almost constant rumination on the pros and cons of the journey, the anxious-making, moment to moment wondering that I cannot shed, the what-if thought of suicide always somehow there, lurking in the darkness of the moon-cratered mind, the final answer to any painful question, the one perfect out. I was not surprised in the least when Elsie's father told me my mother had taken the pills intentionally. And when Bumby blew his head off, I was absolutely devastated but definitely not shocked, and unkindly one of my initial thoughts after hearing the news was, You beat me to it, dear brother, now I have to stay behind to deal with the aftermath, damn you.

One thing I can say positively for Stuart is that he unwittingly helped to keep me alive these past few years. For the narcissist loves the idea of a suicide—not his own suicide but the self-death of his partner, which is incredibly exciting for the narcissist, all the so-wanted, grief-stricken attention coming his way, the thrilling sexual fantasy that your beloved has given her whole self at your altar, reflecting her devotion in the tombstone of forever, this is the ultimate jerking-off for these sickos, all of this according to so many of the books I've unfortunately forced myself to read on the subject.

"When did you know that you liked girls?" I said.

I asked Elsie this after she made me taste her chardonnay. She said, "One sip won't hurt you, I'll let you know if you're stepping over the line, Scotty Legs."

"I so like being called Scotty Legs—and I don't know why. Maybe it's because no one has ever given me a nickname before."

"You should give me a nickname, too."

"Elsie Eyes," I declared, proud of myself for coming up with it so quickly.

"That's pretty lame, but hey you're new to all this play."

"Really? I thought I nailed it."

"I've always known I liked girls," Elsie said, skipping ahead, and I must say I was rapt listening, this was all so new for me, I felt so privileged and excited to hear any intimacy she might offer up. "I was on the soccer team in middle school. And there was this other player, Kylea, and we were always aware of each other, you know. We were coming home on the school bus from an away game, at Larchmont, and we were sitting next to each other and we just began to kiss, to the astonishment of all the other players on our team and the bus driver. too."

"Oh, my God, that's so courageous. How old were you?"

"I was fourteen, but I already knew the world was one barbaric lie. Kylea was so scared, and sadly she was also the one who paid the price—I didn't. My father was cool with everything. But Kylea's parents, when they heard what happened, they freaked, they sold their house and they moved across the country and they put Kylea in a new town and a new school, I shit you not."

I had no such brave story to share, no sweet first kiss to tell about, Elsie was my first love, I had lived as a message in a bottle, floating on a remote ocean, endless endless, will it ever end, a vacant horizon of blue, would anyone ever uncork me or would I simply drift on forever, a tiny unseen bobbing. It was only in my chaotic dreams, in the threadbare fantasies of self-pleasure, or in the solitude of my study, engrossed in the novels of others, that I would give sporadic mind to my truest self. Every morning striding to work, striving to look busy and accomplished, I found it impossible to resist those quick, side-long glances at the other striking-looking women of Fifth Avenue, even if I was ashamed to hold my gaze—what an insane life we make for ourselves. Good for you if you have it all figured out, have found your true self and your true love, because for the rest of us it can be as bleakly hard as a winter in Stalingrad, a cold spell so endless and empty making even the notion of hope feels like a flickering, burned-down candle, almost gone, all gone.

I think the reason I have always lived inside novels is that for me they were the safest places I knew to explore gender and sexuality and the splintered voices that breathe in all of us. In the world outside, they ban books and they burn books, yes, they heave them in murderous piles and gasoline them, and they call you a witch and they look for a stake to light if you are gay and a Jew, tell me now if that's not all true. My father changed his name from Bromberg to Dorian not just because he loved a certain nineteenth-century novel, and think of poor Oscar Wilde, even, his brilliance such a threat to the unbrilliant, the barbarians and executioners in plain sight everywhere, they will never go away, history tells us that repeated story more often than any other. It still felt ridiculously brave to kiss Elsie in a fish shack in the United States of America.

Chapter 25

In the late afternoon, Dalton asked for the keys to my father's old Saab, a 900 Turbo, which was in the garage and which we fastidiously maintained, keeping the battery charged and bringing it in for regularly scheduled tuneups, as if someday my father might somehow reappear and take the wheel again.

Dalton insisted that Elsie and I join him on his errand. We had already granted Hawk the day off—and he was off somewhere in the Rover. It was drizzling lightly when we got into the purring car, the seat warmers already warm, its backward Swedish wipers in intermittent mode, the tan leather interior still smelling of my father's cologne, Paco Rabanne, the ghosts of the past with us always.

Dalton had wanted to pay our respects at Leo Gross's grave, which was in Montauk on a wind-swept hill looking out over the white-cresting Atlantic. Dalton spilled out a bottle of Jim Beam at the foot of a pink marble slab that said: "Leo Gross, 1945-2011. Losing $5000, That's Almost Like Winning."

"Leo loved to play blackjack," Dalton explained, shaking out the last few drops of bourbon. "That was the motto of that detective, Joseph Reaper, in that hardcore series of his. Truthfully losing five grand would've killed Leo. He liked to take the ferryboat out to Foxwoods. He played three-dollar blackjack. Drank bottom-shelf whiskey, cheapest bastard you ever met. Lorraine, his third wife, once told me that he would never eat at any restaurant that didn't have an early-bird special."

"This is such a pretty little cemetery," Elsie said, spreading her arms to it, her gorgeous black hair gusting about like a flag in the wind.

It was, just a couple of acres, no more than a hundred gray stones, most of them older and moss scarred, a nice spot to contemplate eternity from. It made me think of the first chapter of *Ironweed*, William Kennedy's career-making novel, the dead speaking from the ground, from their wormy entombment, strange how often my memories came from the soil of books, more within reach than my actual living memories.

"Old Indian cemetery," Dalton explained. "Leo claimed his great great grandfather or somebody another was from the tribe. Crock of shit. Leo had his eyes on being buried here for years."

"I didn't even know you liked Leo," I said.

"I like him well enough now that he's dead," Dalton said. "I still think that soon-to-be ex-husband of yours forged those found Reaper novels. The only book Leo left unpublished was this godawful period piece about fur traders, back in the seventeen-hundreds, half of it was in French, thing was about eleven thousand pages long, every publisher in known existence had turned it down. He made me read it, son of a bitch."

"Most authors have an unpublished in their drawers—and it's usually there for good reason."

Dalton took out another pint of Jim Beam from a pocket of his time-softened corduroy jacket. "This one's for us," he said, passing the bottle around. I respectfully took a small sip, while Dalton and Elsie each took a couple of deep gulps.

"I brought you all up here for a reason," Dalton said, wiping his mouth with his jacket sleeve. "I know you thought we were just being our usual literary-tourist selves."

"Literary tourists is our special phrase for visiting the graves of famous authors," I told Elsie. "We do this sort of thing a lot. By the way, have you been to Baltimore yet to visit F. Scott and

Zelda's joint grave? We should do a road trip soon, I can show you the house he occupied there in the nineteen-thirties."

Elsie said excitedly, and oh, how much I liked that she said it with such quick enthusiasm, "I would love to do that with you, Scotty. I've seen the images of the gravestone online. They use the *Gatsby* inscription, 'So we beat on, boats against the current, borne back ceaselessly into the past.'"

"Probably one of the most quoted lines in history," Dalton said sourly. "I absolutely despise it. It's what John Lennon—now there was a fine writer, we had a hell of a night once in Los Angeles, but that's a whole other misbegotten story—it's what John said about McCartney's song 'Yesterday'—pissed him off for the same reason, all this sentimental hogwash that everything lies back in the rearview. Pathetic, man."

"I don't know," I said meekly enough, "I've always loved that last sentence to *Gatsby.*"

"A lot you know," Dalton said. "And I mean that, child. For example, did you know that your freak of a husband attacked Sadie about six months ago, he actually picked up a cleaver in the kitchen and threatened her with it, that's a fact beyond disputing."

"How come this is the first I'm hearing of it then?" I said, feeling a rush of fear, the familiar and anxious dread that accompanied anything having to do with Stuart.

"It's because you don't sleep with Sadie, as I do on many occasion," Dalton said without pride. "Sadie didn't want to alarm you any more than you already are. She knows you've been a basket case and she didn't want to add to your troubles. And I heard the thing about the scissors. Stuart standing over you as you were asleep, good thing Sadie was looking out for you, otherwise who knows what could've happened. What a nutjob, I still have no idea how you ever fell into it with this maniac."

"This coming from a man who has been married six times, mind you," I said more to Elsie than to Dalton.

"Why do women like you so much?" Elsie asked Dalton.

"They sense that I can protect them," he answered thoughtfully.

"What are you going to do to protect Scotty from this man?" Elsie said.

"How long have you been having occasional sex with Sadie?" I asked, desperately wanting to change course.

"Ever since your dear father got tired of her," he said. "That's just another thing you don't seem to know. Where have you been all this time, Scotty? It's all right fucking in front of you, don't you see."

The rain was picking up, the winds were turning to gusts, but somehow I didn't mind the cold splatterings, I deserved them. Elsie was sweet enough to huddle close, to put her arms around me.

"I think Stuart killed Leo," Dalton said. "I don't have any fucking proof, just a ripe hunch is all I have, but I think he killed him, just the same. Georgie told me, yeah, in bed, what of it, that she believed that he had altered the contracts with Leo's estate, upping percentages, giving Stuart total control, who knows, I certainly don't know, but there you go, make of it what you will."

"I thought Leo died of natural causes," I said, confused.

"He drowned, they said he had some kind of cardiac arrest, all bullshit, if you ask me," Dalton said. "Leo didn't like to swim. What's he doing in the Atlantic in late September, this is a guy who worried the hot tub wasn't warm enough, no way Leo suddenly decides to take a goddamn dip in the ocean. Bet your bottom dollar Stuart has something to do with it, not that I'm the shamus to prove anything."

"I don't know, Dalton," I said, huddling with my girlfriend, there, I said it, as the wind and the rain continued to whip us. "You've never been wrong, as far as I can tell, not ever once."

Dalton winked at me and gave me a yielding smile and then he said, "Scotty, you know what I've been really thinking the whole time we've been here, and if you were thinking the same it would not surprise me in the least. I've been thinking about the old novelist William Kennedy and those Albany marvels of his, what a supreme master of time and place, and more to the point I've been thinking about that first chapter in *Ironweed*, what a great American novel, he wrote the one and that's all you ever have to do, isn't that the truth, dear daughter?"

"Don't I know it, Dalton. I pray he's still alive and writing and enjoying this life," I said, tearing up as I surveyed the rainy-day gravestones, thinking that all of our names will one day be stonily inscribed, sooner than we ever believe.

Chapter 26

Elsie and I made energetic love when we got back to the house, which is not surprising after visiting a graveyard. She loved me, though, in the way I have always wanted to be seen, and that was most surprising, to have my absolute secret wishes and funky desires fulfilled, I did not think it would happen in this life, what had previously been barren like the endless feel of Nebraska prairie, to have met all unmet expectations so that I could actually die now without lowly regrets, that is the power of good sex, the only equal of which is a good novel. Don't let me die yet, God, not yet, not now, at least wait until the book is finished, don't take me before, this is my simple prayer, I'm still a work in infinite progress.

What a tender sweetness to be in her arms, breathing her in, her hair damp with sea rain, her skin tasting of rose water and jasmine—when she was not looking I spied her fragrances and cleansers, how I liked that we shared bathroom shelf space, held them to my nose, inhaling with wonder, this body next to mine—all the while the cozy patter of rain on the roof and at the windows, how romantic—how trite that word is but it had been in such short supply for me that I feel entitled to use it—yes, romantic, to be in the fire light, under the down blankets, for once feeling safe and cherished.

I uncurled myself from Elsie, after she had fallen asleep, pausing only to look at her supine beauty for a moment, like rereading a perfect sentence, how is something so wondrous even possible, let me reread it again, thank you, God.

I would be in the study watching my mother on my laptop screen when Elsie found me next, quietly sobbing as I had for the last hour. I had been wanting to find the right preserved moment to watch the video of my mother that Shane Gregory had shot with his first-generation VHS camera just before she died. It felt no different to me than if the large radio telescope arrays of SETI had suddenly circuited to life with the grainy transmission of extraterrestrial intelligence arriving millions of years after the initial feed.

I know you want to know what my mother said to me, and that I'm not inclined to share it will bother many of you, you'll think it is a cheat, since we live in an upheaval of Tweeted obits and Instagram families, as if we are to weigh in on every single unprocessed thought and feeling, our Facebook postings like an obsessive, ongoing Kerouac stream, that there are no insignificant moments in the social conscious of social media, our last step before our chip-in-the-brain future, all of it, the last french fry you ate, the last movie you saw, your last heady fuck, all of the parts equal in this zero-sum game, and that we should all needlessly check back on one another in five minutes, to see if anything has changed since last we clicked and checked, and here I am a few minutes later, and nothing has changed for me, I'm still not wanting at all to tell you about my mother, more than ever I want to keep it for myself.

I will tell you two things, though. One is that one of my authors, a well-regarded futurist, has written a book called *The Last of Us*, which details what the post-Singularity world will look like, this Kurzweilian nightmare, the last humans, the post humans, our merging with machines before we become coded entities that live forever in a snow-globe virtual universe, and he tells me this is a hopeful vision for us—I don't think it's saying much to say I want nothing to do with it. I asked him what the future of literature looked like in his imagining, and he said there was no future for it, that information is just bits and that novels with their complicated, spurious emotional landscapes would hinder our forward progress, as we evolve and leave humanity behind.

The futurist actually said, "It won't be possible to understand, let us just say, a Jack Kerouac fifty years from now. It's all unsteady, unreliable, druggy emotions, and we're moving to a place where nobody in their right mind, and with the absolute choice, would want to feel the things Kerouac felt like feeling."

The satisfaction I didn't yet possess at that moment was that Stuart would be dead by tomorrow evening, his murder as grisly as anything the tabloids have ever reported on, and that he would miss out entirely on the immortal future, just as my mother had missed it and everyone else who will die before this so-called Singularity. All was not completely bleak, though, as I contemplated the life growing within me, my son—I determined that I was carrying a boy, I just felt his strong, directed purpose— this boy who might never grow old and die, who might never visit a cemetery, a son who would carry on our brave, family traditions, one way or another he would make sure that there were novels in the next evolution of mankind.

The second of the two things I wanted to tell you was that when Elsie discovered me at the laptop and saw my mother's lustrous face on the screen, she devined instantly my deep suffering, and without intruding knew to sit down beside me and to put her arm around me and to kiss the tears off my cheeks. Then she took my hand and led me back to our bed.

There is actually a third thing I need to fill you in on, it's not that I forgot, it's that I wondered if I should start a whole new chapter. The placement of information is always key for both the author and reader, and it is preferable to avoid trickery, though sometimes real life falls in ways that dominoes do not, practically defying the laws of our normal physics. I apologize in advance if you will also feel the same quick succession of shocks that I was stung with.

For it was only a few hours later, as Elsie and I were in what we called the family room—which was different from the living room and the grand den and the game room—with Sadie and Dalton, the blue-stone fireplace ablaze, illuminating the nautical bric-a-brac, oars and duck decoys and ancient lobster traps that qualified as decor, making even the pizza boxes and chianti bottles seem warm and homey, as we had decided to make it easy tonight, although Dalton did make a rather serious play for dinner at Nic & Toni's, pleading with us that the ricotta gnocchi and Berkshire pork chips, along with their Yukon golden potatoes, were calling out to him, his memory for menus as detailed as a thirteen-year-old boy's recall for the statistics on baseball cards, I remember Bumby astounding me with lifetime batting averages and career total hits, even though he always performed poorly in math class—where is this going, you are rightly thinking about now—but there we were, pizza and wine, fireside, the sizzle and pop of the well-seasoned wood, and playing the hardest fought contest of Scrabble in perhaps the history of word games, just think of the participants, everyone was a writer and a lover of vowels and nouns, even Sadie, who surprised me with her quick erudition, later, much later, years later, she would surprise the whole world and write a great book about me, she called it an autobiography, as famous as the one that Gertrude Stein wrote for Alice B. Toklas, *The Autobiography of Scotty Dorian* it was indeed called—in the middle of all of this, at the stroke of midnight, the East Hampton police rapped on the ancient brass knocker of our medieval front door, and when this was met with silence, they hit the doorbell, which was rigged to ring in every room of Sonny Weebler's sea cottage.

We were greeted by a gangly young officer, still with acne—I'm not sure why I'm wasting valuable sentence time even describing him, but I did think in this surreal moment at the door how he didn't look tough enough to be a cop, that he would never make it on the city force; also I should admit now that I would have many unkind and unjustly-likeminded thoughts in the days ahead, that the shock of unexpected death, multiple deaths, in fact, would bring out the worst in me, as if I had been permanently unchained from propriety—anyway, the acned officer asked if we knew a person who went by the name of Hawk. The GPS in the Rover, we learned, had been programmed to this address.

The short of it was that Hawk was in critical condition. He was brought to Southhampton Hospital after he was bludgeoned from behind with a crowbar, the bloodied tool was found near Hawk's broken, unconscious body, in the parking lot of a motorcycle-dive bar in Amagansett, I'd tell you which one but I don't want to invite any more lawsuits. There were no witnesses, apparently no one had seen anything unusual—nobody seeing anything—Nope, I can't say I did, I'll let you know if something comes to mind—would be an ongoing refrain in the coming days. My first thought hearing about Hawk was of that menacing private investigator, Lee W. Heany, which I decided to leave at the door unspoken.

According to the emergency room doctor we would talk to at the hospital later that night, Hawk's skull was fractured, what we were told was a compound depressed fracture, and there was a very real risk of hemorrhaging of the brain, which would probably necessitate surgery. Hawk also had multiple broken ribs, which actually seemed more like a petty afterthought from the assailant.

Elsie and I sat vigil together in the sickly fluorescence of the waiting room, it was four in the morning, oh my, I was tired, hospital waiting rooms are the same no matter what time of day or endless night, though, a place where clocks cease and cell phones are drained of their incessant energy, where our own lifeblood drains, removed from all that we thought was so mightily important just a small while ago—the harried job, the thorned relationship, the status quo—all under the watchful eyes of God, as we ask for forgiveness and redemption and hope and, yes, we promise to be much better people if only, if only, please save him, please save her, please save us all.

Elsie and I were disbelieving but trying to keep cool heads, we tried to keep it light, we read to each other items in the ancient celebrity gossip magazines that were piled germ-ily about, Elsie read an interview with a now-dead talk show host about his "iron-clad rules for living," which was a hoot, considering he was no longer living, all that B-12 and grass-fed beef means very little in the end, and I discovered a sensational cover about Jack's secret homosexual lover, this porn star in the valley, what a crock, but it made us think about Jack and we called him in Beachwood, and of course he was now already on his way, what an absolute winged angel, I was so glad it was his baby in me, of all the possible men in the world.

It was decided Elsie would remain in East Hampton, staying close to monitor the situation with Hawk, while I would helicopter to Manhattan to attend the Crop Duster's service later this morning and deal with Stuart in the afternoon. When Elsie and I parted at close to six—I did need to take a shower, after all, and change clothes—she simply said, "I think it was that detective in the Stetson, he did this to Hawk, I'd bet money on it, what do you think, Scotty Legs?"

Chapter 27

Less than twelve hours later, after two hours of fitful sleep, a missed funeral service, and an afternoon spent inventorying Stuart's belongings, we were in J.G. Melon, a hamburger joint on the Upper East Side, at Seventy-fourth and Third, an easy walk from 1040 Fifth, fifteen minutes or twenty minutes, depending on your gait, no more. We needed to be in a busy place where we would be seen, and Melon's, noisy with chattering preppies, the kind of pink-button-down-tartan-tie clientele who would surely know our names and social status, was a perfect match for what we were up to. Dalton wanted to go to Daniel, Boulud's fancy French restaurant, but Sadie and I and Susan Ogden argued that it was not the right choice for our particular mission, even though Dalton pleaded his case, with all the upright integrity of an Atticus Finch, arguing for their Ossetra caviar and Scottish grouse and Quebec suckling pig, it would be wrong not to give into temptation on this particular day and to even celebrate a bit, he concluded, our faces as stony and numb to his defenses as jurors deliberating a capital crime.

We all ordered the same thing, Bloody Marys, mine a virgin of course, rare hamburgers, cottage fries, all classics—I thought it slightly ironic that this was Stuart's favorite lunch stop. J.G. Melon had been occupying the same wood-paneled, pressed tin-ceilinged, checker-tabled space since 1972, its lovely green awnings and its name aglow in pinky-red neon out front, as much an institution as anything is these days. I was grateful to be in a room that I knew so well, its wall pictures of watermelons always brought a smile to my face, my father and Bumby and I must've dined here at least two hundred times over the decades, I tried to make an accurate count, anything to occupy my scramble-egged mind, all I knew was that time-honored familiarity was most needed at this extreme moment.

We were told to exhibit gaiety, the highest of spirits. Did I tell you my very own Jack Kerouac was by my side? He looked so handsome, he wasn't dressed like Kerouac today, he was in Hollywood black, what designer I don't know, but the shirt was a shimmery white and the suit was slim and the color of charcoal. Seeing him, seeing his outrageous beauty, gave me high hopes for our son, good looks are such an advantage, as easeful as having money. Jack had flown in on that same studio Gulfstream that Elsie and I had enjoyed only a few days ago. I was glad to see so many of the customers doing their best to surreptitiously point Jack out, their eyes on our happy and privileged table, the grass was so much greener over here with us.

We kibitzed with waiters we had all known for years, Jack took lead here, what a charmer, and Dalton held court and told, complete with Irish brogue, what would usually be a funny story about the death of Seamus O'Leary:

"So the old village priest says to the townspeople," Dalton recounted, "won't someone come up and please say a few words about our dearly departed friend and family member? Silence. Not a fucking word. The priest says surely there is someone here who has something to say about Seamus O'Leary. More silence in the parish church. The priest says, Frankly there has to be someone here who can say something good of this man's life. He lived with us, he was one of us, he loved with us, ate with us, prayed with us—surely someone can say something positive of this man.

"The silence continues to be deafening. All right, the priest says, we're not leaving this church today until someone says something good about this man. A voice from the back cries out, 'His brother Paddy was worse!'"

We all laughed crazily, and I had heard this before about people in total shock, that the natural emotions you'd expect after a great trauma, such as grief and shuddering disbelief, go anything but the normal way—for example, bringing on unsuitable fits of hilarity. Sadie sucked back more of her Bloody Mary, tears of laughter screaming down her cheeks—and, here's the truth, she had just snuffed out the life of a man, and she had done it no differently than in the way of stamping out a used cigarette. Susan Ogden, who had never been known for her sense of humor, neither as a man nor as a woman, could barely control herself, as she slammed her fist into the table repeatedly to say, "Oh, my God, that's rich, Dalton."

Susan incidentally had my husband's severed organ in her Tory Burch handbag. So much to talk about, you see. Yes, you heard that right, Stuart's penis was in her chic white leather tote—and he was dead, not that I knew how this would end, none of us did, but I will let you know now that the bodycount was far from finished, isn't that a crazy hoot, so many more inappropriate tears of laughter to come.

I had made sure not to have any face-to-face contact with Stuart, and I was sitting anxiously in my living room when I heard a terrible thud and cry come from Stuart's study. Let me back up just a wee bit, beeping much like a United Parcel truck. We missed the Crop Duster's service, sadly, unfortunately, there you go—he was dead anyway, he would not care one way or the other, another of my newly minted unkind thoughts. Dalton, Sadie, and I arrived at the East Hampton airport at the appointed morning time, we had even boarded the six-seat helicopter, our sound-defeating headsets donned, the thirty-five-foot rotor was spinning and whomping—but then all the fury came to a silent stop.

Lightning and thunder boomed and zigzagged the horizon. We were told there would be no helicoptering until the storm passed, and the latest meteorology reports put that at many hours away, so we gratefully accepted the charter company's offer of a chauffeured Mercedes limo to the city, which often can be done in one-and-half hours but most unfortunately for us this morning, not just with rush hour but with multiple highway accidents caused by the slick road conditions, and which seemed to take forever to be cleared, our journey took over four hours, closer to five, actually, come to think of it. Of course, I got a most relished chance to catch up on my sleep, as Dalton and Sadie spent tender time together, I was now most aware of their ancient kisses, Dalton was right, what a dolt I had been, how could I have missed all of this, I mean, I had my suspicions, but I didn't let those glimmerings set into deep knowledge, how could I have missed so completely Sadie's long-running affair with my own father, where have I been is right, how self-occupied am I.

Knowing we had missed Hendricks's service, we made our way directly to 1040 Fifth. Once there, we simply waited for Stuart to make his last appearance, not that any of us knew it would be his last, certainly that would qualify as premeditated and all of this I can assure you was most involuntary.

As I said, I sat by myself in the living room. Sadie, Dalton, and Jack told me not to worry about a thing, which is probably when I should've started worrying, we've got this covered, they assured me, easy as cake, *no problemo,* Jack actually said, they would watch over Stuart and Susan Ogden as they did their inventorying, yes, Susan had arrived with him, I should've guessed, the couple they had once been and who were forever more to be. I quivered and cowered in the great room, hoping that it would soon be over, waiting for someone to let me know that they had finally left when at last I heard some shouting, soon followed by that terrible thud and cry. Even then I remained impassively in place, on my favorite couch, until Jack yelled out for me.

I ran to my husband's study, where everyone stood mutely, in what was a tight circle, they parted an opening when they grasped my presence. Stuart was lying prone on the Persian carpet, the one he had so carefully chosen to match well with Leo Gross's writing desk and kingly chair, his head bashed in, the heavy, orange IBM Selectric—not quite the murder weapon, as you shall see—on the rug beside him, blood spewing from his nose and his mouth, a gurgling, gulping sound bubbling up from him, he was still breathing, still very much alive, there was no doubt of that, although no one had yet made a move to do anything remotely life-saving.

We stood over him, just errantly watching, not a one of us—Sadie, Susan, Jack, Dalton, and I—reacting for what felt like the longest, most insane time.

I finally broke the spell, "Shouldn't we call 911?"

Before anyone could answer me or pull out a cell phone, Sadie—her eyes gleaming with a kind of directed knowledge—grabbed a throw pillow off Stuart's couch and then she crouched down next to him, placing the pillow over his face and then proceeded to suffocate the very last breaths of life from him, and none of us did anything to stop her, such was the karma of this man, such were the chains that he would carry later.

"He was never going to stop," Sadie said, standing over Stuart's lifeless body.

What a jumble. I would learn that in Stuart's last few minutes of life, before he had been savagely hit with the typewriter, that he had been complaining, and rightfully so, that his filing cabinets had been broken into and that his Traveler, the one Dalton had been using, was missing. Stuart howled out not at Dalton, or even Sadie, for these offenses but at Susan Ogden, who had finally heard enough. With tremendous and magnificent might she grabbed the Selectric from Stuart's coffee table, lifting it ceilingward, how strong she suddenly was, and in one swift, unrepentant motion smashed his head in.

Jack told me Susan's words, immediately afterward, were, "That's enough from him, don't you think. What a complainer."

But as you know, Stuart was still gurgling and alive, when Sadie reached for the pillow off his couch.

There we stood, Dalton, Jack, Sadie, Susan and I, without a clue about what to do or about what would happen next. I said nothing, neither did anyone else again for the longest time. Then Susan said, "I don't think we should leave this in the hands of the police. Sadie and I are not fit to do jail time at this point in our lives. Also, I think there might be many questions about why the three of you, Dalton, Jack, and yes you, Scotty, failed to take any action to help Stuart."

What a freakish, bastard child of a moment, standing over Stuart's corpse, all of us trying to make a sane decision—but how could I ever hurt Sadie, the mother I never had? Likewise Dalton would never hurt her, and likewise that, Jack would never hurt me. Susan and I had the same light-bulb moment, it was time to call Carlo Bassi, who else would believe this scene we were in, who else would know how to write ourselves out of it.

Susan seemed to have no trouble making this peculiar call, she was Carlo's literary agent, I thought you knew that. Carlo, as he liked to say, owed her a great great deal, she had made all of his literary dreams come true, which for him, as he also was prone to saying, was even better and more satisfying than the sacred Mafia oath he took to become a made man.

Susan kept to the facts, it sounded no different to my ears than if she was negotiating percentages with a foreign publisher for rights, that dry and unencumbered. Now I knew Carlo really had lived a life where these kinds of messes were quite ordinary, he loved to tell Susan and I about the fucks-ups of doing business, as he called it, the hits that went wrong from beginning to end, the lunacy of how some people refused to die, the gang-that-can't-shoot-straight moments that seemed to befall every job, all of the treacherous insanity that had worked to give him the material and starting-off point to become a fabulous writer at middle age. I'm sorry to say Carlo would not get to finish his second novel, he too would be murdered within months, his body unfound for many years, he and his bodyguard executed by an old rival, their bones finally discovered one fine day in the future in sealed drums at a New Jersey waste-disposal facility, so brutal an ending, so completely irreconcilable with his graceful words on the printed page.

Carlo was fully alive now, though, and he instructed us to exit 1040 Fifth, to look jokingly happy for all the world to see, and he further instructed us to go to the nearest busy restaurant, to continue our merry-making party, let him handle the rest.

Before we could leave, though, Susan seized the letter opener from Stuart's desk and, with a truly demented smile, as if she wondered how she had not thought of it earlier, ripped open his fly, I can tell you none of us saw this coming, she took his thing in her hands, you know what she did, you know the rest, I had to turn away, somehow it made her feel better, what does it matter, sick as it was, dead is dead.

Chapter 28

The DeWitt Wallace Periodical Room, named after the founder of *Reader's Digest*, once a benefactor of the New York Public Library, hearkens back to another age, to one so much more dignified and culturally ambitious than our own. It is a baroque masterpiece, a fabulously ornate quarry of European marble, skyscraper walls of mahogany and ebony, bronze chandeliers and oaken tables and walnut chairs, a reminder of the great private fortunes that once allowed us our reading leisure.

The long, polished reading tables had been turned into banquet tables for tonight's festivities, long on our calendar, the annual Library Lions soiree, Dalton is one of the honorees and had even committed to read from his new memoir as one of the main attractions for the check-writing donors, a black-tie and silk-gown swirl of lifted faces and lifted eyebrows who had no personal need for the use of a library but were certainly not above the notion of a once-a-year gathering of fellow swells, their photos splashed in the *Times'* Sunday Styles section, associating with noble books and the starved authors who toiled to write them helped to bring a certain luster to their own money, which in most cases was not so nobly gained.

The giant murals in the periodical room depicted the once-and-gone glory of New York publishing, Charles Scribner's Sons and Harper and Sons, the McGraw-Hill Building and the Puck Building and the Hearst Building, the artist Richard Haas rendered these imposing facades with a most respectful palette, taking his brush to ordinary brick and mortar to create great, glowing literary cathedrals, such anachronisms, as if anyone held them in near-holy regard anymore, this library palace that I had loved so as a young girl only made me sad nowadays, all was rushing forward at an unblinkered pace.

What a week it had been since we murdered Stuart. The obscene thing was Kent's novel had sold out in a single day and we were rushing to do a second printing, all of Kent's shiny dreams of bestsellerdom had finally arrived but just like the Capote epigraph to *Answered Prayers*—"More tears are shed over answered prayers than unanswered ones"— you have to be careful what you wish for, perhaps Kent, at the moment the most famous author in the country, was also pondering the wisdom of Saint Teresa of Avila from his cell on Rikers Island, certainly Capote was a literary hero of his, perhaps even someday Kent would write his own twisted version of *In Cold Blood*, in fact I know he would.

Kent had been charged with Stuart's homicide—seemingly already convicted and sentenced in the halls of social justice, and to judge by the comment forums, aflutter as they were that it was a waste of the taxpayers' money to even have a trial, the YouTube video so damning and incendiary, over ten million views, last I checked—like I said it had been quite a week, such suspense I've never known, such brilliant, page-turning work by Carlo Bassi. I certainly didn't see this one coming.

We started out with cocktails in the Edna Barnes Salomon Room, with the grim portraits of Astors staring down at us, as if even they smelled a rat. Elsie and Jack accompanied me as my dates, and Sadie joined Dalton as his, what precocious new times we were suddenly living in. We all caused quite a stir tonight, the camera bulbs exploding like blue grenades, as we stepped past the famous marble lions at the library's entrance, Patience and Fortitude, making our first public appearance since the news of Stuart broke across the lightning storm of all media, flashes across the wide empty horizon, search-engine bolts heard in every corner of the land. I made sure not to smile as these would surely be photos that would never go away, more endless emptiness in this pixel book, coded by ones, our life stories now being written by machines. Currently we were trending hotly and we would still exist in cyber in the far distant future when the last humans continued to tap names into databases, I knew I would show up every time someone clicked on a title of Kent's or Leo Gross's or Dalton's, or even Jack Kerouac's, we were all linked together like Lucien Carr and David Kammerer and William Burroughs, how my Jack liked those dark glowing linkages, all of us now in the eternal engine.

In the first couple of days after the murder we heard absolutely nothing, not a whisper, not a breadcrumb, the world continued to go about its tired business, it was as if the whole thing had not happened at all. Carlo Bassi had called us at the end of our meal at J.G. Melon and he said simply that the coast was clear and that it was safe to return to 1040 Fifth and that he would take particular care with all the rest of it, whatever that meant, though later as I've said we would understand and we would marvel at the literary flair and creative genius that Carlo had brought to the assignment.

When Sadie, Dalton, Jack, and I returned to 1040, the body was gone, disappeared like a magician's trick, the apartment had been wiped forensically clean, not a foreign hair follicle, not a drop of blood, it was just as it had always been, only better. Let me say what should now be obvious, I was airily glad that Stuart was gone, I actually slept like a feather-goose dream all week, even the niggling anxieties of police inquiries and being found out seemed pale in comparison to what it had been like while Stuart was still alive, the heebie-jeebies of that minute-by-minute insanity of having to wonder whatever would he do next, how lovely to have my mental shelf space back, may he rot in hell—what, were you expecting that I'd turn contrite and ask God for forgiveness? Should I follow all the established literary norms and mores of what the protagonist should be feeling and saying and doing after the savage murder of her husband? I mean, even if he deserves it—

and Stuart surely did deserve his brutal end exclamation point—
the conventional thinking goes that I should still possess a kind
of tragic remorse, edit myself into the wounded, broken heroine, a
universal survivor, the long perspective, giving into that profound
sense of grief that transcends all of us, what it is to be a human
being, what evil lies in every man and woman, that in the very end
we are all stained and culpable in such a thing, yada yada yada.
After all, Scotty—I can hear it in my head, what the book's editor
will say—we don't want you seeming too cold and black-hearted,
we don't want to lose the reader now, think of all the good, hard
work you've done to get us to this point.

Dalton, like me, also seemed to be in a great, fabulously
unrestrained mood. He had finished his memoir, only yesterday,
and that meant high, champagne spirits. He said, "What's the
plan for publishing it?"

I said, lifting a flute, what a no-no, but we were celebrating,
"It's my big book for the summer, I'm putting the entire machine
behind it, the hell with everyone else."

"Yes, that's it, dear daughter," he said, clinking me.

Elsie, who looked ravishing in one of my Vera Wang gowns,
said to Dalton, "Why do you always call her daughter?"

Before I go any further, it is crucial, even betrayingly sad, to
note that I have not shared any of the backstory with Elsie, and
neither has Jack, not a twitter about what had happened at 1040.
Elsie is as believing as everyone else, all she knew was the talk
of the town, that Kent had taken bath salts, a street drug that
increases sex drive but sometimes also leads to psychotic, violent,
even cannibalistic behavior. It hurt not to be able to share with my
Elsie what had really happened, I so did not want to have any lies
between us, even ones of omission, which are of course the most
giant lies of all.

Dalton, looking spiffy in his tux, more Papa Hemingway than
Hemingway himself, answered, "Scotty Dorian is a better daughter
than anyone in my life, including the two flesh-and-blood ones
who are supposedly from my seed. I will continue to call her my

daughter, that will not end."

If Dalton had declared that he was my real father, I would not have blanched, and if the blood tests had revealed it, I would've been most fine with it, he was a dear father in this family of my own making.

Elsie said, "That is a beautiful thing to say, Dalton. I'm so glad you are in all of our lives. And I'm so glad we're all together tonight, I know this has been such a difficult time for everyone."

Dalton actually winked at me, the happy wink of co-conspirators getting away with murder. The first few days we had to play it so cool, all of us going about our muted routines, Dalton typing his epilogue, finishing up the story of his life, Sadie making hearty beef stews, like witches' brews, casting a warm spell on us, Jack making his excuses to movie producers, calls to the coast that no longer crackled long distance, as clear as calling to the next room, me checking in with editors and agents and authors, a roster of the ordinary, all of it what should be, how it would seem if Stuart was still alive and going about his own business.

A few days into it Elsie was able to leave Hawk's bedside—he was improving rapidly, beating the odds, isn't that wonderful news—to join us in Manhattan. She accompanied me to my new obstetrician's office, where it was confirmed what we already knew. I was a young pregnancy in an old body and I was given guidelines for diet and the usual questions for a new mother first expecting, nothing that couldn't be sussed out on the internet, but reassuring nonetheless, all looked to be in working order. My doctor asked if I felt any changes to my body, and I said, yes, my breasts already seemed plumper and that in the mornings my mouth tasted of the metallic, nothing unusual there, either. The doctor thought that I should probably opt for amniocentesis when I came to my sixteenth week, to screen for abnormalities to the fetus—that's when I stopped her right there and told her I was having this baby one way or another, that my baby was absolutely fine, and I did not need any faulty, dangerous tests telling me otherwise.

It was a whole three days of our ordinary routine before we heard

anything at all. And the first news was not even about Stuart—
Georgie called to tell me that Stuart's private investigator, Lee W.
Heany, was found dead in his rented Chevy Volt, in a derelict part
of the Bronx, in what looked to be a drug deal gone bad, he was
executed, a bullet to his hammy head, traces of the same bath salt
drug found in his car were later found in Kent's own bloodstream,
a synthetic chemical called cathinone, which derived from the khat
plant, the tabloids were full of this information later, how helpful.

Two days after visiting with the obstetrician, four whole days
without knowing a thing, where was Stuart's body, exactly, how
would all this be revealed and come to light—well, that's when
Kent, naked and savagely confused, came out of his Greenwich
Village apartment, painted in Stuart's blood and screaming
unintelligible things, all caught on the now infamous YouTube
video, titled "Cannibal Author," made by a passer-by on her
Android, all the evidence anyone really needed.

When the police entered the apartment that Kent and Stuart
had been sharing they found the bath salt drugs and a scene of
such dissected carnage that one veteran detective was quoted in
the headline dailies as calling it, "HANNIBAL LECTER'S LOVE
NEST," Stuart's dismembered body was found everywhere, in the
kitchen, in the bathroom, pieces of him sawed off in a frying pan,
all of it so gruesome the whole country was retching and relishing.
There was even coverage of Stuart's missing penis, the speculation
in the chat rooms was that Kent had enjoyed it as an appetizer,
it could not have been big enough for a whole meal, ha ha, what
passes as humor and discourse today, will we ever find our way
again.

It did not help Kent's defense, either, that the police detectives
also found notebooks and index cards in Kent's own hand,
purporting to show the plot lines for the recovered Leo Gross
manuscripts. Along with a laptop that had never been plugged
into the current of the web, several Hermes Rocket typewriters of
early-nineteen-sixties' vintage, and several dozen reams of a paper
milled in 1978, it seemed certain that Kent was not just a drug-

debased cannibal but a book forger, as well—from that moment forward he was also a bestselling novelist, I guess that is what it takes these days to grab the public's wayward attention.

Carlo Bassi had outdone himself. How much I wanted to know, how had it all been accomplished, how was even the body removed. Witnesses appeared out of the ether, a neighborhood drug dealer who swore that Stuart and Kent were some of his best clients. Even Darren, my own doorman, had given an interview about seeing Stuart leave our building, describing him as being "in a pretty upbeat mood, when I think about it," which is strange since Stuart most certainly left 1040 that day in a downbeat, dead mood.

To really bring home the point of how well-crafted Carlo Bassi's thriller was, it turned out that one of Leo Gross's newly released novels, ostensibly one of those forged by Kent, had a subplot about a terrible new street drug called "Beast" that turned people into, yes, you already know, flesh-eating cannibals.

We made our way from cocktails, leaving behind the snooty portraits of the Astors, all privileged eyes still on us, to the Periodical Room and the dinner honoring this year's Literary Lions. Jack was nowhere to be seen, he had been hijacked by fans from the moment he walked in, how difficult his life was, his fame quite a burden, even if he handled it with deft aplomb, the real Jack Kerouac had died under its harsh lights, nowhere to run, so much expected of anyone who can write such staggering sentences, the American disease of expecting our authors to be something like their books, nothing anyone can live up to, the same with actors like Jack, everyone has their own bizarre internal interpretation.

Elsie shook my arm and said, "Oh my God, look over there, it's Kerry Hudelson."

Kerry Hudelson was the third richest person on the planet, a search engine creator, in his thirties, handsome in the way of all those autistic geniuses from Mountain View, his hair unruly and unassisted by the help of any stylist, his body gaunt and lean, not because he worked out, more as if he had no patience to eat or even think about such basic, subsistent living.

"Neighbor of mine in Montana," Dalton said casually. "His million-acre ranch, second only to Ted Turner's two-million-acre ranch, adjuncts my six acres. I taught the rich bastard how to make trout flies and fish, he's practically a buddy of mine, even though he's quite weird, spends his precious time immersed in something called *World of Warcraft,* video-game stuff I don't understand, nor do I really want to at my age, but I'm the one who gets credit for inviting him here tonight."

"He has about seventy billion dollars in his personal piggy bank," Elsie said, looking at Dalton with something verging on awe, as if she understood his particular genius for the first time. "Perhaps he'd like to buy half of a great publishing concern, do you know what I mean?"

"Exactly my point, dear daughter," Dalton said to Elsie. She actually clapped her hands in glee and then high-fived both Dalton and myself.

It was actually that easy, Hudleson was a die-hard fan of Elsie and Jack's show, later at dinner they regaled him with behind-the-scenes shenanigans, and it turned out that Hudleson was still smarting from losing his bid to Jim Irsay, the owner of a National Football League team, the Indianapolis Colts, who walked away with the first draft of *On the Road* at a Christie's auction, which Kerouac typed on a continuous roll of paper without paragraph breaks in the year of 1951, which to most of you must seem like a million years BC, this one-hundred-and-twenty-feet of tracing paper that Kerouac had taped together and that fit neatly into his battered typewriter, for this Irsay paid $2,200,000, more than all the money Kerouac would earn in his living lifetime. Kerry Hudleson had bid only a hundred-thousand less for this curiosity, advised by a trusted advisor who is no longer advising for him, but here's the thing, he was still bothered by losing out on that particular piece of literary history and he was ready to make his next major bid.

Dalton suggested without any hard sell whatsoever, with the

same tonality as he might use asking anyone to cough up a few bucks for coffees, that the multibillionaire cast out a line, flick it out far, perhaps throw down three-hundred-and-fifty-million real dollars, well above our anticipated purchase price, to buy Martin Cage's one-half stake in the company.

The autistic billionaire said to this, "Will do, got your meaning, Dalton, I'm sure as heck not going to miss out on anything else that matters."

What an evening, all was so fine and good, finally. Dalton even thanked me in his speech. He said the real reason he was back to being a writer was me—that I was the hero of this story. The chapter he read aloud from the stage had me tearing up for all that was lost, it was about my father and mother and their great love affair, I don't care even if Dalton was making it all up, let me tell you, just to sit there, between Jack and Elsie, to hear Dalton Ford's transcendent words, so generous and loving towards my parents, Irwin and Elsie Dorian, the truest patrons of the arts, he declared them, lauding them for eternity in a way that they could never have imagined, since they would be gone, Dalton would still be here, and their memories would be held by a drunken author who always had a way with words, the final curator.

I was like a wriggling trout, I thought—looking across the table at the billionaire angler Kerry Hudleson, who nodded with evangelical fever, so rapt as he listened to Dalton, the real old man and the sea, Dalton's reading no different than if he was offering his voice to God, a God who probably was just another besotted fan—who had gone after the silvery, glinting lure, who had gulped big and sunk my teeth into a shadowy illusion, all was lost and as my fluttering and crazed body came up to the sunlight and air, the old fisherman took the hook out of me and said, I hope you've learned something, go on now, enjoy the rest of your life, as he threw me back and I hit the clean cold water again, the miracle of where I'd already been but only now could so appreciate.

Epilogue

Assistant District Attorney Dana Ashcroft, one of five hundred prosecutors in the Manhattan district attorney's office, had longly waited for her moment, you could hear it in every razored sentence, sharp clean swipes at our stubbly defense. Dana, with her crisp Bennington good looks, she had studied English literature there, not only that her mother had been a runner-up for Miss America, there wasn't a thing that seemed unknown about Dana, it was said she ate hot oatmeal with chopped apples and raisins every morning, what dedication, it was all ruthlessly documented in the tabloids, they dubbed her the "Prosecutor Queen"—well, Dana understood that this was her time to make a shiny name for herself, cases like this just didn't come along every day, you have only one chance at it, like a first novel, and if you blow it, you don't get to write another one these days, that is all there is to it, deal with it, I have had to.

Dana had proven herself a brilliant researcher, the talking legal doofuses on the nightly shows—I finally had to buy a television—put her ahead in the count, she had built a methodical, nuanced case against me, a monotonous escalator ride of forensic evidence and mismatched timetables and worse, that woeful autopsy report, all backed by the devastating testimony of her star witness, Susan Ogden.

Our defense had rested and Dana was finally getting a chance to give her closing argument, surely it had been rehearsed and edited at least a hundred times, there wasn't an excess word, not a false dramatic note, she was managing to beautifully bolt down all the loose contradictory pieces into place like the mechanical cylinders of a complicated locking device finally all clicking at once, the forever-jarring clank of the Rikers cell door becoming permanent.

The twelve jurors and two alternates, who had stared at me with an unrelenting sameness for the better part of three months, not exactly a look of grimness but certainly not friendly, more like fellow travelers on a subway car that had become unaccountably stalled and delayed, were at last beginning to show themselves, the look of terminal impatience was giving way to moral outrage as Dana struck repeatedly at the salient truth, which was that a living person, once my husband, no longer lived.

"Scotty Dorian," Dana said, jabbing her finger in my direction, concluding, "is nothing but a storyteller. This is who she is, a fabricator of reality, from a long line of fabricators. She could not tell the truth if her life depended on it, as it certainly does now. This is what novelists do, they don't live with us in the present moment, they are the resisters and destroyers of reality. I submit to you that Scotty Dorian murdered her husband because it was great material for a book that she will now have plenty of time to write from behind bars."

Ouch, got me there. Oh, please, my dearest reader, you didn't think, really think there was a trial, do you—or did you now? I did indeed buy my very first television, though, that was real, Elsie insisted, and I must say I'm glad I did, so much good writing on shows these days, so much that is worthwhile, nice to sit on a couch, just the two of us, immersed in the same material, calling out our revisions at practically the same time, always looking to make the dialogue better.

There was no trial for me, there wasn't even a trial for Kent. He pleaded guilty, temporarily insane he admitted, had no idea what he was doing, recalled nothing at all about his cannibalistic assault on Stuart, didn't even remember his own addiction to bath salts, but it had to be true he thought like the rest of us, since he too had seen that YouTube video, he plea-bargained himself down to ten years, he'll be out in six, he took the deal, Kent certainly did, on the advice of his lawyers, he told me all about it when I visited him at Rikers, how exciting to be looking at him through the unbreakable glass, just like on TV, Kent seemed pretty much okay, at least not on suicide watch anymore, and he was already beginning to staple together the stray thoughts and notions that would become his next novel. Now all that is well and good, but of course I will admit to a huge dollop of guilt here, after all, we all know Kent is an innocent man, that should still count for something. Poor, lonely Kent, enduring something like out of Kafka's *The Trial*—what am I even accused of, he must ask at his root, how is any of this at all possible?

He still yearned for Stuart even, what a moony fool. He did not yet roller-coaster down with Stuart on the dark-rage machine, all Kent would ever know were the sweet, drunken times, all his next novels would be love letters to Stuart, disguised as murder mysteries, Stuart would surely have liked that, more adoration at his grave.

Of course it was all made possible because of Susan Ogden, a woman scorned. It turns out it wasn't Carlo Bassi who plotted out the revenge on Kent, as talented as Carlo was, he was not that good. Susan and Carlo had talked, and she was the wizard of the narrative, she had read so many books by now, it was second-nature to her, she had no idea of her true gift, all those crime and detective novels had seeped into her blood, she could twist and turn with the best of them, and I'm sorry to report to you that she wouldn't get the chance to write her own series of procedurals, she took her own life and we'll come back to that in a short moment.

Susan must have struggled, as I did, with Kent languishing in a cell on Rikers, hard for any of us to be blithe about, a true prisoner's dilemma. I mean, Kent was the bottom to my own husband, to be crass, and I know that Susan hated Stuart for his new affair, funny though how she could accept me in the bed of the man of her dreams but took it out on Kent, a sweet, discerning writer who deserved better.

You know, I struggled with my own prologue, how it was stealing from Kent's sad plight and misfortunes, setting it on Rikers, on burial duty, of all things, but wow, what an opening, it was such a hook, and I knew it, and I didn't know how to retreat from it. It's what brought you here, and I knew my prologue had to be over the top, and it was—I mean, come on now, rich people like me don't go to prison, silly. I tried to rework the scene to give it more realism, with me wearing an ankle bracelet in my Fifth Avenue apartment, house arrest, but that draft just turned out laughable, million-dollar lawyers and me, a rich-bitch client, eating take-out from Shun Lee Palace, you've already lost everyone, you see.

Susan cut her wrists on the steps of the ornate mausoleum that Stuart's hedge-fund father built for Stuart on a grassy hill in Green-Wood, in front of the blank-eyed stone angels, and she was found there with her manuscript, an eighty-page suicide note, a work of great fiction, which not only exonerated Kent but all of us really, she told her truth with such verve and exactitude, detailing how she and Carlo orchestrated the whole thing. She left out the part of 1040 Fifth—Sadie, Dalton, Jack and I, we did not exist in the story of her own telling, which I'm grateful for, of course, what a nice way for Susan to let me know that she never meant me any harm.

Susan's manuscript was believable enough—by the way, the entire suicide note was printed in *The New York Times*—to get lovely Kent out of prison, an early release, I can't tell you how glad I was for that. As the blood slowly left her on those stone steps, giving Stuart the reflection of forever that every narcissist desires, she also left behind his shriveled-up penis in her new Dooney & Bourke bag, which was enough for the police and the regular citizenry to call it a day on this one.

Since he was released it has been reported that Kent is often seen on those same cold steps in Green-Wood, with a lunchtime sandwich, looking like he is loopily talking to himself.

Perhaps he has been driven truly mad by these events, hard to say, hard to ever know such things, but I often wonder about those missing days immediately after we killed Stuart and whatever was done to Kent. Georgie Guns handed in her latest Nicoal Angel thriller only a few weeks ago, it's called *Vow of Silence*, and it is as they say a book pulled from the headlines, at its dark heart is the savage killing of a lawyer named Steven, whose male lover is set up to be found wild-eyed and dripping in his partner's blood on the city streets, yes, another cannibal on bath salts.

"I'm sure you'll be intrigued by my latest masterpiece," Georgie had said to me over cocktails at Bemelmans, the bar in the Carlyle Hotel, one of my favorite old-timey Manhattan haunts, though that night it had been at Lizza's suggestion—yes, she's back at work, good as new, not that we ever talk about her extended stay in Bellevue's psyche ward, sometimes the politest thing you can do is just to make believe it never happened, most people are all too quick and happy to go along with that plan.

"Scotty, you know what's funny," Georgie said without humor after her third martini, "is how everything worked out so great for you. Look at you, richer and more powerful than ever. You have the love life you've always wanted. The lawsuits died with your husband. Even that sociopath private detective Lee W. Heany wound up with a bullet in him, how nice for you again."

"Such strange coincidences," I said, bringing my martini to my suddenly dry lips, wondering anxiously where all this was going.

"I guess," Georgie said, not sounding convinced. "You know, you're like one of those rabbits over there—" Here, Georgie pointed to the great, whimsical wall murals that Ludwig Bemelmans, the creator of Madeline, those fabulous children's books, had painted so long ago in the bar in exchange for lodging at the Carlyle, what artists will do and have always done for their art. "Like a picnicking rabbit in Central Park, without a care in the world, how swell to be you, Scotty. Like I said, I'm sure you'll find my new novel most intriguing."

Georgie's novel is quite fascinating on many levels. It describes almost to a tee what happened in my apartment the day of Stuart's murder, indeed Georgie has taken the wild liberty of setting her own fictional murder in the limestone edifice of 1040 Fifth Avenue. All very strange, since Georgie of course wasn't with us that fateful day—is it the thrill of artistic license, or is it something much worse? Is it at all possible she was staking out the apartment that afternoon? I am most certain that none of us have ever said anything to her because we have taken our own vow of silence.

The apartment at 1040 Fifth Avenue, in Georgie's novel, belongs to Brett, the ravishing daughter of a prominent Manhattan attorney who has recently died of a heart attack, leaving the family firm to her. Brett's husband is a sociopath who wants to cheat her of her inheritance. Incredibly, the murder weapon is the father's old typewriter. After Steven's murder—the result of a domestic squabble gone insanely out of hand, they were arguing about the last time they had sex, which did strike me as kind of funny—a desperate phone call is made to a mafia chief that Brett is representing in a murder trial, talk about conflict of interests.

Georgie goes into excruciating detail about Steven's body removal and the clean up. I found this chapter way too exacting—there was unneeded information on the particular solvents used on the Persian carpet and she even swerved away to give a heavy technical demonstration about how to disarm security-camera footage into an endless, pointless loop—in fact, I will surely suggest edits.

Anyway, within an hour of the call to the mobster, an emergency medical services vehicle pulls up to 1040, followed right behind by a police cruiser with fake cops. The standout moment here is the doorman being brought into the back of the cruiser at gun point and told that if ever utters a word about what he is seeing then he can say goodbye to his twelve-year-old daughter. Of course the fake cops somehow already know pertinent details about this school girl's schedule, what fiction, the bad guys are always so bad, still it gripped me and if anything

I will suggest only a few tweaks to make it more believable.

Now this brings me back to Kent. I have, as I said, continually wondered about his missing days before he is discovered painted in blood in the notorious YouTube video. Georgie's stand-in for Kent, whom she calls Trent—who knows, maybe it will help to sell copies, I won't insist that she change it—is just grabbed off the street in broad daylight by thugs in a nondescript van.

Trent is shot up with drugs for the next seventy-two hours to the point of incapacitation. This is by far the toughest stretch of her book. He is mostly unconscious, in and out of delirium, without any muscle ability to defend himself. Trent is held in a Russian gangster's brothel, where he is raped countless times, over and over until he is driven quite mad.

I don't think Georgie's new book is much good because it is much too concerned with finding out what she would probably call the truth, for lack of a better word. Great novels are their own truth, they just bring us in, there is little need to ferret out the details, their worlds are so much bigger than ours.

I was considering all of this in the dreamy, mad sunshine of a perfect October day. We were on an excursion, doing our own little bit of literary tourism, we had started at my house in East Hampton, where we are spending more and more of our time these fresh, new days, and then we drove around the Great Peconic Bay to the ferryboat at Orient Point, the crossing to New London over the sparkly undulations of Long Island Sound, and from there we took the highway up through the old-industrial heart of Massachusetts, ordinarily not the most thrilling of rides but it was peak foliage season, the colors astonished, a crimson and golden splashing over of God's champagne, we were all drunk on it and on each other.

Dalton was at the steering wheel of our princely new Volvo, in a color the dealership described as Burst Blue Metallic, as my father's antique Saab was no longer sufficient enough for our growing family, though of course we continued its cherished upkeep, and Sadie, Dalton's soon-to-be wife, sat beside him in the front-passenger seat, as it should be, while the new prince slept in the back, in his tiny car seat between Elsie and me.

Not too far outside of Lowell, the birthplace of Jack Kerouac, we stopped at a highway rest stop for a picnic lunch. Sadie had outdone herself, lobster salad, the best pate, buttery soft cheeses from the remotest French countryside, baguettes from the corner bakery this morning, a whole roasted free-range chicken, homemade sausages, on and on and on—she would make a good partner for Dalton, she understood his needs, which were actually few and mostly having to do with digestion. Dalton, for his part, had packed a basket of the finest wines, he iced bottles of rose champagne, how nice of him to think of me, we would refuse nothing today, but I would insist that Sadie drive after lunch. What a warm deep feeling inside, to guzzle bubbly while breast-feeding my baby, my, oh my, how my world has changed.

Dalton said, "I think we should skip the cemetery. Be a mob scene today. Not much to look at, as I remember."

"Not true," Elsie said, she was so gorgeous in her wide sun hat and yellow sundress. "Used to be true that they just had a flat marker at the Edison Cemetery. But they added a large commemorative stone a few years ago. It's made of Vermont granite, it's six-feet wide, eight-inches thick, and weighs three-thousand pounds. The inscription is simple but I think right: 'The Road is Life.' I want to be there and feel Jack's presence, if it's okay with you, Dalton. I came prepared, too. I have a map, he's in Lot 76, Range 96, Grave 1. We'll make it quick, but I need to be there and pay my respects. He gave me life with my TV series."

"You fit well into this family," Dalton said after a long postponed moment. "You are a true literary tourist. Although I will say I would rather just opt for the pub tour, that sounded like the best thing on the schedule today. I remember some of those bars, the Old Worthen and Cappy's Copper Kettle, they were all Jack's style, nothing fancy, all low-key, I never really understood the fellow, to be truthful."

It was something to watch Elsie and Dalton engage. *Dalton*

Ford's Moveable Feast was on the *Times'* bestseller list and it was sure to earn him another Pulitzer, all the reviews crackled with adoration and love for his long, endured road, he was a national treasure it was now declared, and Elsie would have her first novel out, *Nat and Scott*, I was so grateful to publish it, before Christmas, already the advance reviews were a marvel, she would be famous, too, in a new form, and I would help to guide her so that she did not lose her self along the way.

I was so excited, too, that we would be reunited with Jack today. He was the star attraction at the annual "Lowell Celebrates Kerouac Festival." My Jack had become an even bigger glowing in the sky this past year, as his movie version of Carlo Bassi's first novel had not only exceeded all commercial expectations but seemed a golden carpet ride to the Oscars, we shall see, we shall see, but I knew how proud all of us were of him. To accentuate this newfound maturity, Jack asked me to hold off on publishing his novel, he wanted to take another pass at it.

Elsie said to Dalton, "What is it about Jack Kerouac you don't understand?"

Dalton continued to pour glasses of the pink bubbly while somehow gorging on a rosemary chicken breast at the same time. "Well, here he is, all those years of struggle, of eternal wandering, and he finally makes it, big time, the dream of every writerly lad in the land, and he keeps coming back to Lowell, half its businesses boarded up, the economic good times gone, no different than Northport in the day, it's as if he could never escape what he came from, like a sad salmon that kept going home to die.

"Look at me," Dalton continued. "I have no problem living with you and Scotty and Sadie on Fifth Avenue and in East Hampton, this is why I trudged all those years. I haven't been back to Bozeman in how many months is it?"

"Bozeman, Montana is not exactly hardscrabble," I interrupted. "I can't wait, we'll all be there in the spring. You and Kerry are going to take us trout fishing, remember?"

Sadie said, "Yes, Dalton, you promised all of us. It will also be a wonderful celebration of you landing number one on the nonfiction lists."

"It's the wrong list, you know that my book is monumental fiction, as I keep telling you all, if you'd only listen. I think the only one even trying to pay attention to what I'm saying is baby Irwin."

Yes, our baby is named Irwin Kerouac Gregory-Dorian. Elsie has told me that she thinks I'm putting a lot on this very young man. He is the most loved baby ever. With Elsie, Sadie and I, and even Dalton, not to mention Jack, picking him up at every free instant, no goochie-goos from this crowd, just ruminations on the literary life, wrong turns that we hope this baby will avoid, so that he may do better than us, oh, please, my sweet little darling Irwin, find your way without so much of the tumult.

The stop at Kerouac's cemetery plot was quick, as my Elsie had said it would be, there was quite a crowd there today, their stray offerings of Canadian Club and Budweisers beginning to look more like the stackings of a delivery truck than the tender personal offerings at a grave.

Dalton drove us—yes, he kept driving, he is most obdurate, as you all well know by now—by Jack's boyhood home, the directions from memory. Then we all met our Jack in Kerouac Park, in downtown Lowell, not far from the confluence of the old mill rivers, the Merrimack and the Concord, we had views of nineteenth-century mill towers, these same sights, in fact, are described in Kerouac's first novel, *The Town and the City*, a book he was never quite proud of, at least how it was finally printed and released, edited in ways Kerouac never gave permission for, which informed every word he would write later, and no one, but no one, would ever get to touch and fiddle faddle with his words again, his trust in the world was forever lost.

It filled my heart with a warmth that brought wetness to my eyes to see Jack hold baby Irwin close to his brawny chest, this glowing man, so much larger than life than any of us have ever known, he would never let anything bad happen to his child, who also just happens to be mine, too.

Kerouac Park appeared to me like Stonehenge, alien pillars of granite in a regular grassy, American park, all these carnelian columns in a kind of circle, all with carved-out quotations from Kerouac's books, perhaps in the far future it would also be a cause of wonderment to whatever replaces us.

Dalton put his arm around me and baby Irwin, as if he already knew where I was, which he most certainly did. He said, "Reading these granite quotes is like reading *Gatsby*, it's all in the past. Look at this one, you know it and you've heard it before, but listen to it, and you can hear all the musical strains and voices that made Kerouac Kerouac." Dalton then read off the stone:

So in America when the sun goes down and I sit on the old broken-down river pier, watching the long, long skies over New Jersey and sense all that raw land that rolls in one unbelievable huge bulge over to the West Coast, and all that road going, and all the people dreaming in the immensity of it, and in Iowa I know by now the children must be crying in the land where they let the children cry, and tonight the stars'll be out, and don't you know that God is Pooh Bear? The evening star must be drooping and shedding her sparkler dims...

Dalton's voice trailed off, as if he had suddenly remembered the man who actually wrote it, his old friend Jack Kerouac. "On one level, what poetic chicken manure," Dalton said, snapping to. "On another more sentimental level I do admire the ceaseless past and that we all belong to it."

Somewhere in the future there would surely be a park in Montana named after Dalton Ford, and I would most likely be the one funding it, but I was hoping that that park would be a long way off.

Dalton said, "You see, my darling daughter, and my darling grandson, what we learn to do every day is to die a little bit. We're always readying ourselves for that last moment, when as Jack says the sun goes down and we all sit on the old broken-down river pier. Jack had written everything he needed to write and that's why he was blessedly allowed to leave us, there was nothing more he had to say, he was smarter than the rest of us. Fact is, the only reason I'm still around is that I've still got something to learn and I'm still transcribing it for the rest of you idiots."

Jack, Sadie, and Elsie joined us in front of the granite column. Nearby a paisley hippie girl with a guitar had attracted a small crowd of the other literary tourists. She finished up singing Dylan's "Blowin' in the Wind," then sequed into the Beatles' "Paperback Writer," which seemed right considering Bob Dylan and the Beatles had affirmed Kerouac's impact on their words and music and life journeys, I guess the singer knew all that.

My Jack touched the inscribed words on the column before us with a kind of reverence and said, "The last sentences from *On the Road.*"

Sadie said, "You know what my favorite last sentence in literature is?"

We all turned to look at her in the last blazes of sunshine. "Dalton wrote it this year," she said.

Elsie knew it. *"I'm Dalton Ford, and I have lived a life,"* she said most dramatically.

Dalton said, "What sanctimonious crap. I just wanted to be done with the thing and get my money. I'll tell you a great last line in literature, it's Joyce's short story 'The Dead,' you know what I'm talking about, *as he heard the snow falling faintly through the universe and faintly falling, like the descent of their end, upon all the living and the dead.* Now that just can't be beat. Although he gave it a good shot with *Ulysses.*"

Jack said with actorly power, *"Go, my book, and help destroy the world as it is."*

"Good one, Jack," I said. "Russel Banks' *Continental Drift.* I've always loved the last line of *Catcher* myself:

"Don't tell anybody anything. If you do, you start missing everybody."

"Scotty, you're such a sentimental sap," Dalton said.

As much as the first sentence in every novel should be amazing and bring you to the second sentence, the last sentence in the book has a different kind of importance, don't imagine for a moment that I haven't been thinking about it for months.

I have no *Gatsby*-inspired last line. Unlike Fitzgerald and Kerouac, I don't believe "in the green light, the orgastic future that year by year recedes before us." Truthfully, I'm quite optimistic about what comes next.

The last sentence of a novel should matter. The reader shouldn't want all of it to come to an end. As a novelist, if you've done it right, the reader will enter the search engines and look for all else you might've done, clicking your other titles on Amazon, getting them ready for check out.

Just as I had struggled with the first line of the novel, I had struggled with the last line. My first attempt, which only took about three weeks of staring at a blank screen, was this:

From my perspective, I'm glad all of this nonsense is over. Although I'm not sure what I'll do tomorrow.

I know, I know, a bit too glib and a touch too cynical. My editor said it sounded well enough like me, but that it wasn't quite good enough because I had overpromised the reader and built it up so much. He was right, of course. All of us novelists want our last sentence to pack not just a wallop but for it to distill whatever wisdom we have accrued not just in writing the book but that reaping of an entire lifetime, talk about an impossible challenge, what ego to even attempt it.

My editor gave me some solid advice, he said I was trying too hard, and that if I was like most novelists I had already written my last sentence. He told me to reread the manuscript and that it would be shining up at me like a nugget of found gold. He was right again, how ever did he know. I had written it early in the book, at the very end of Chapter Seven, the first time we are in Bernie's bar, The Last Columnist.

It will never ever be good enough, you have to know that I know that, but it is the right sentence, and it seems just as appropriate to use it here, as it did earlier in the book, standing together now with my family, how much I dearly loved them, how precious they are, how sad it makes me to know that these kinds of moments must be savored because we never know how many more chances we'll get, Dad, Mom, Bumby, but today standing tall among Kerouac's Stonehenge pillars in the last, fading glorious golds of late afternoon, hearing the beginning ripples of John Lennon's "Imagine" from the paisley hippie girl—a song that Jack Kerouac never got to hear because it was recorded after his death, how strange my mind is, always thinking wayward things like this— Dalton already beginning to argue for a favorite old steakhouse nearby, if we hurry quick we won't miss the prime rib special, Elsie argues back that we are trying to veer away from red meat, nonsense, Dalton proclaims, he wants horseradish and dripping roast beef with baked potatoes and real sour cream, he remembers too that the clams casino and lump crab cakes are worth the trip all by themselves, Elsie shows resolve and holds to her position, such stubborn beautiful people in my life, Dalton wins her over by telling her we'll do something vegan tomorrow, which I know he'll never do, but my wifey husband falls for it anyway, now the soft yellow light is disappearing, almost gone, all about to become an elegiac blue, now we are just shadows on the monuments, as we reflect on literary immortality and contemplate black eternity, everything reduced to a single never-good-enough sentence:

Every great pop song, every great newspaper column, and every great book cries out, I was here once, I lived among you and I made my mark, now it's your turn, see what you can do.

ACKNOWLEDGEMENTS

I would like to very much acknowledge the contributions of the following people for sharing so generously and warmly with me, over the ever-quickening decades, their personal memories and experiences of Jack Kerouac from his time in Northport, Long Island, covering the period of 1958-1964: the photographer and architect, Lawrence Smith; the owner of Gunther's Taproom, Peter Gunther (1934-2016); and the painter, Stanley Twardowicz (1917-2008). I want to especially thank Larry for access to his amazing photographs and recordings of Jack, which—along with my own family's relationship to Kerouac—helped bring him to life for me. Of course Kerouac's own writings tell us all we'll ever need to know about the man.

Sterling Lord, Kerouac's literary agent who was also fortuitously my father's agent, continues to represent the published works of Mike McGrady—and we remain grateful. I would also like to thank my own literary agent, Daniel Strone, who has represented me for over three decades. Thank you, Dan, for striving to make sure my own novels would see the dappled sunlight of print.

Sean McGrady, a long-time resident of Northport— a small town on the north shore of Long Island that Jack Kerouac also called home—now splits his time between Olympia, Washington and the California Bay Area.

Mr. McGrady had four novels published with Pocket Books in the 1990s— three of those novels were recently reissued in new trade paperback editions by Simon & Schuster. The critically acclaimed Eamon Wearie series includes DEAD LETTERS, SEALED WITH A KISS, and TOWN WITHOUT A ZIP.

THEY DIED IN VAIN, a book detailing the best and most overlooked mystery novels of the last century and edited by Jim Huang, describes the Eamon Wearie series as "emblematic of life in America at the end of the twentieth century."

Critic Kate Derie says the characters are "well drawn and vivid" and that the dialogue and settings "ring true" and further describes federal agent Wearie as retaining "something of the best idealism of the best private eyes, a man who is not himself mean although he walks the mean passageways of Postal Depot 349."

Publishers Weekly simply declared, "McGrady's prose scores."

SLEEPING WITH JACK KEROUAC is Sean McGrady's first new novel in over twenty years.

PHOTO COURTESY OF NICHOLAS MARAVELL
ORIGINAL COVER ART BY NICHOLAS MARAVELL

COVER DESIGN BY LINDA WOYTOWICH

Made in the USA
Columbia, SC
24 September 2017